Hydrophilica
Gretchen Van Lente

Alternative Book Press
2 Timber Lane Suite 301 Marlboro, NJ 07746
www.alternativebookpress.com

Hydrophilica

Originally published in electronic form in the United States by
Alternative Book Press.

Publication Data
Gretchen Van Lente [2018]
Sisyphus/ by Gretchen Van Lente—1st ed.
Ask Publisher for Further Publication Information

ISBN 978-1-940122-39-7
Printed in the United States of America
10 9 8 7 6 5 4 3 2 1

I tell my neighbor that Allen Ginsberg and Bob Dylan once stopped over my house for trick or treat on Halloween but she doesn't believe me. I tell her this happened years ago, but the memory of it is still fresh in my mind. I say that Bob dressed as a giant Snoopy Dog and that Ginsberg dressed as a fairy. She says she knows Bob and has met Ginsberg and that could never happen; they wouldn't do that. Now I have to ask myself if I hallucinated the whole thing.

I am so obsessed with it I want to ring Bob up and ask him, didn't you once trick or treat at my door in a giant Snoopy Dog suit? I could give him my address and have him verify that. And what sort of superb friendship did you have with Ginsberg, I would ask. How lucky you must have been. How sad you must be at his passing.

For in spite of my neighbor, and she would know, I haven't given up on my theory, that tired of being closeted with his fame, Bob Dylan put on a giant Snoopy Dog suit and with the less recognizable Ginsberg went door to door collecting candy until, right around the corner from his house, they came to my house, where they startled me.

There is plenty of evidence against me, I mean in favor of hallucination as opposed to a real Bob in a real Snoopy Dog suit, the real Ginsberg dressed as a fairy to poke fun at himself, I have to imagine.

My own record shows that I have a schizoid affective disorder. If I don't take my medicine I hear voices that say, "Shut up Bitch! Eat your mush or I'll kill you!" But I take a lot of medicine, and still I have panic attacks every day.

Without the medicine—and I don't take it like I should—I see things. Once I saw my neighborhood on fire. I live on a cul-de-sac, and when I stepped into the road, there was an umbrella of orange light covering all the houses, which were being licked on all sides by melon colored flames. Black smoke billowed over the roofs. I started down the street but a fireman stopped me. This road is closed, he said sternly, staring me down. It was only when I returned to my house that I thought how strange—the fireman dressed in fire gear from the fifties—just exactly like you would find in a child's book from that era. Like a favorite book of mine when I was a child, called Fireman Dick, about a small child who is rescued from a burning tene-ment building by a firemen. In the picture book Fireman Dick wore a long rubber coat and a brimmed helmet with a large shiny badge on the crest of his hat. Fireman Dick is smiling as he carries the young boy down a long ladder while pretty flames roll over the roof like icing on a cake.

I sat inside my house all day waiting for Fireman Dick to arrive smiling at my door to evacuate me. Tired of waiting, I walked outside. It was a beautiful, clear day in Malibu and my neighborhood looked pristine and perfect with its man icured lawns and lush gardens, its wealthy homes and its rotund mansions. I had dreamed the whole thing up with my eyes wide open.

I once saw a woman with a tail. I was walking down the street toward the post office when I spotted her, trying to

tuck the tail in under her skirt. She would walk a few steps and out would pop the tail, something big and bushy like a lion might have. Something, if you could imagine, with a mind of its own. She would walk a few more steps and stop to tuck it in again. I caught up with her and looked in her face. To make things worse she had elephantiasis in her legs and couldn't shuffle fast enough to get away from me. It occurred to me that she might be a circus performer, but that would not account for the look of mortification on her face as she ducked inside the post office, presumably to lose me. I followed her in, but when I passed through the door she was gone. As if disappeared. I still walk that beat looking for her, thinking that sooner or later she will come to retrieve her mail or post a letter.

My dreams are no less strange and no less real to me, full of intricate detail and color. Some of them are waking dreams. I could be doing some mundane chore such as sewing or washing the dishes and I will begin to dream with my eyes wide open.

Some of my dreams, I know, are centuries old and it feels just as if I have been sleeping for many decades, waking by mistake in the present century. In the morning when I wake I know beyond a doubt that I have visited the past--as an ambassador in the court of Queen Elizabeth, say. Or as a domineering clan leader among our primate ancestors.

Once I fell into a coma. I knocked my head by accident on the sharp edge of the cupboard above my kitchen sink, and afterwards I went to bed and when I woke I was not myself, not comfortably inhabiting my bed, but living in a swamp at the north end of Malibu. I say *in* the swamp, for I was no longer merely human. I was human in parts but more than that I was a selfish, rapacious monster. Slimy and saurian and aquatic, with an unappeasable appetite for human bones. In this life, which is more real to me than reality, my scales become dry and brittle and they litter the swamp with dander the size of dinner plates. A sign that I am growing old in monster years. My breath is dragon strong, and I smell partly of burnt flesh and partly of the feted swamp where I live.

There are so many dragon flies out on the swamp that it looks like an infestation. They couple and fly together. Bull frogs get to be the size of opossums. They sound like giants in a belching contest. Opossums are the size of wild dogs. The water rats look like skinned cats. All of these taste about the same since I devour them so quickly. They taste for a moment like something hot and fleshy and then they are down the chute, and I hardly feel like I've eaten anything. Domesticated pets sometimes wander in from the sparsely planted houses up in Decker Canyon. They come to explore the lake but they never leave. I have a weakness for these well fed pets. Catching them is so easy it's like picking berries. But again, they only whet my appetite. It's humans that I like the best. Without a human being to eat now and then I would never have survived five hundred years, and I will live into eternity if I can supply myself with enough victims. If not, pity me, because unlike frail humans I have no after life. When I die I will only be dead, and there's not another like me anywhere in the world. Not even in the universe, peopled with lizard extraterrestrials as it is.

I have supersonic ears and I am a mind reader if I set my heart on it. It is merely my animal intuition. I can reshape myself and slime my way into cracks and crevices or I can puff up and bloat like a frog for the sole purpose of making myself look more horrific. Looking horrific is a natural defense. Or should I say offense. People freeze at the sight of me, and then I devour them without the least bit of resistance.

The lake is my mirror--a black mirror. I stare at myself for hours, marveling at how plain horrific I look. How scary and treacherous. On that subject I am vain. I have, if I breath in slow and deep, a royal neck ruff like a great queen. It rises up behind my back and circles my head, spreading open like a fan with sharp jagged points. I have a snout pressed into my face and a thick brow like an ape, with worry lines. I am iridescent green when I am not cam ouflaging or molting. I have a crest of spikes which runs from the middle of my forehead to the tip of my snaky tail. But the curve of my back is human, and I sit up on the rocks humanly. The roundness of my mouth is pretty and petite, very feminine, as are my hooded eyes which are glassy and black and shaped like almonds.
My fingers are webbed and my nails are sharp red talons—in all other respects my fingers are human, except that I use them offensively to slice through the soft tendons of my victims.

My happiest memory is of startling the girl. She was

twelve in human years. Her name was Ivory, and she fished the lake.

She fished with frustration, nervously casting her lines and baiting her hook with something like resentment. She snagged her fingers a lot, and she never caught any fish.

"You're hopeless! You're a Pathetic Loser! Get a grip!" She yelled out over the lake, addressing an invisible some-one. When she was too frustrated to fish, she took a stick and beat it against a tree.

I have a patience which was not human. I lay so still I became inanimate. I took a breath every hour or so. I lay in the tall rushes around the lake and spied up at her. Once she arrived with a man who was not any better at fishing than she was. He baited his hook with snails that he picked up off the ground. That's when I learned her name was Ivory because he called her that, and his voice was full of shame and foolish humiliation. She called him "Dave" but I had the feeling this was her father. She paid him little respect. I had the feeling they were homeless; this was their dinner they were trying to fish out of the lake.

"Ivory," I called out to her one day when she was alone, casting her bamboo pole over the water. I stood up slowly from the shallows of the pool, black water rushing off of me in rivulets of slime and silt. She jerked around. She screamed, dropped her pole and ran. I thought of chasing her down, but I let her go. My basic instinct is as a killer, and I could have killed her father or anyone else who fished out of my lake, but I felt differently about her.

Let me talk about the lake, because I am not just a killer. I have a fondness for things, the lake, for instance, and the girl.

Some people think this is a bottomless lake. There *are* fish in this lake but nobody has ever been any good at catching them. It goes very deep, but there is a soft mucky bottom.   I have lazy spells when I nose myself into the silt and sleep for days or even weeks. It is not impossible for me to hibernate for months, and once I slept for ten years; when I woke I found that nothing had changed but the seasons.

There is a small cave under the lake where I can lay for hours or months or even years, listening to the water dripping.

There is a flock of very terrified ducks here. Why they return to this place, only to be eaten by me, I don't know. I never eat the baby ducks because it's hardly worth my time, and I am careful not to push any of my food sources into extinction. There are tall rushes with cattails; the small lake is surrounded on all sides by a moving wall, as the wind blows almost constantly up here at the top of Decker Canyon, at the north end of Malibu. I say almost. I am able to stop the wind, commanding dead silence when I zero in for the kill.

The girl, Ivory, once cut a path with a machete to get to the shore. The rushes were over her head, so that if I spied on her from somewhere else, for instance, behind the lake in the surrounding foothills, all I could see was her line being cast over the lake above the rushes. But I usually spied on her from shore, closing myself into the wall of rushes. Or I lay under water with my almond eyes staring up through the ripples created by her sinker; I stared at the vexed expression on her face until her image moved away over the top of the lake.

I was surprised, but delighted, when the girl Ivory came back to fish the lake even after she'd seen me. She was in no danger, at the time, of being eaten by me, and maybe this she sensed. She brought, along with her bamboo pole, a thing which reminded me of a medieval crossbow, which she had apparently made for her protection. It appeared to be made from a piece of barrel ribbing, and rubber bands, and a giant metal fork. She kept it at her side the whole time she fished with her bamboo pole. This pole was the size of five of her. She could barely balance it. She dug a hole for it in the mud and watched the water. Her father, "Dave," slept in the sun and kept his pole balanced on his legs. That day Ivory caught a fish because I swam under her line and fixed a big rock trout on her hook. Dave woke and sat up and shouted when she yelled at him. She yanked her line in. Dave scrambled after the fish. He tore it loose, carelessly yanking the hook through the fish's mouth and tearing its flesh open.

The fish slipped out of his hands and fled back to the wa ter, and Dave plunged after it, landing face down in the wa ter with his shirt ballooning out around him. He caught a mouth full of water and gagged and stood up, pretending to look around himself for the fish he knew was lost.

"Oh you clumsy idiot," Ivory said to her father. "Why can't you just fer once get something right!" She was dressed in something like a faded cocktail dress, with torn lace in tiers from top to bottom. The dress came to the top of her bony knees and was sleeveless. The lace was a tarnished yellow. On her feet she wore rubber waders. She slapped her pole back into the water. I swam under her line and fixed another fish on the hook.

"Praise Jesus!" she said when she caught the second fish. "Leave it alone! I'll do it myself! Don't touch it!" she said to Dave, and she waded out in her lacy cocktail dress and caught the fish in her own hands.

Since I was already involved, I decided to follow her that day, to see how she would manage to cook the fish and how she and Dave would eat it.

I blend in perfectly with nature. I can take on the dappled color of Sycamore trees, or the rough chaparral, or rocks covered with rusty lichens, and when I move fast it merely sounds like wind in the leaves. I followed her to a campsite at the top of Decker Canyon, not more than a half mile from the lake. This is why they were fishing the lake, I could see. Why she bothered to come back even after seeing me; it was close to camp, and fishing was her only food source outside of picking wild berries which hardly grew at all up there in the foothill mountains.

I climbed into a Sycamore tree. I stretched myself out along a high branch. I spied down onto the camp. There was trash everywhere. Muddy clothes lying about. Cereal boxes which had been stomped on. Someone had neatly stacked up a pile of cans like bowling pins. The homeless campers lay on the ground sleeping, or they stared up at the sky, doing nothing. Some drank, some smoked intensely, some talked and laughed to themselves and some needled each other.

I could see that, every minute she was cooking the fish, she felt nervous about a man named Charlie, as if she worried he might steal her fish. Charlie dressed in greasy black clothes with volumes of heavy jewelry hanging off his neck and his wrists. He wore strings of fake pearls. He wore large chunks of jade. He wore knotted colored strings around his fingers. He wore a rock around a piece of leather and the rock rested in the middle of his naked chest, as his shirt was open to the waist. His chest was thin and knotted as if he had extra ribs popping out in odd places. In addition, every one of his ribs could be counted.

"When that fish be done," he said while lying down, lifting just his head off the ground. He held the neck of a tequila bottle and stared at Ivory.

"You ain't eaten none of this fish, Charlie," said Ivory. She flipped the fish over, burning her fingers, and I could see she didn't know anything about how to cook a fish. I could see that she had not even cleaned the thing. She had simply thrown it into the pan over the fire. "I told you, this here is fer my father and me."

"Who made that fire you are cooking on, sister! You lucky I let *you* eat tonight." He lay back with his head on the ground, still holding the neck of his bottle. "You tell me when it's done," he said.

"I already told ya," Ivory said calmly, shaking the pan to keep the fish from sticking.

"Tell him!" She yelled at her father, who sat beside the fire with this hands tucked between his knees. He squeezed his knees together and shrugged.

"Tell him this fish ain't for him!"

Her father shrugged deeper. He stared into the fire, glancing timidly at Charlie.

"Well I don't see why not."

"Ha!" yelled Charlie.

"Damn it! I ain't sharing this fish!"

"Is it done?" Charlie got up and moved toward the fire. He pushed Ivory out of the way with his jeweled hand and she pushed him back, but he was stronger, and he knocked her down. She stood up and went for him but he held her off with his hand affixed to her forehead, his long arms keeping her at bay. He laughed as she took a swing at him.

"Leave her alone, Charlie," Dave spoke quietly without moving. He glanced at his daughter with a painful grin; then he put his whole face in his hands. He drew his shoulders in and shuddered.

"Thanks for cooking my fish," said Charlie, and he grabbed both of her thin, flailing arms in one of his hands. With his other hand he grabbed her by the back of her cocktail dress and held her in the air, so that she hung like a puppet. He snorted, laughing.

Dave shuddered. "Put her down, Charlie," he said meekly. He looked up at them briefly and then he covered his whole face with his hands. He peeked out and then he covered his face again.

When Ivory began kicking in the air, Charlie set her down. He grabbed her by the neck and squeezed, choking her. "I *said* thanks for the dinner."

He threw her down and she fell on her back, gasping.

Now I had an interest in what was going on and how exactly this fish should be shared, since I was the one who specifically gave it to Ivory. If she wanted her father to eat some, that was fine, but I was not in favor of giving even a single taste of it to Charlie.

I slid down the tree and waited, crouching in a deep bank of the chaparral behind his back. From there, no one else could see me if I rose up behind him.

Charlie laughed and picked up the pan of fish with a dirty sock. He sat down next to his tequila bottle and began picking at the fish, still laughing. I could see that in his case the evil was every bit as delicious as the fish. I slid out of the bushes. I rose up slowly behind him. Ivory gasped and bit all of her fingers. Dave jumped up and fled, followed quickly by Ivory. They fled down a beaten path.

"What?" said Charlie, watching after them. Slowly he turned around. He gasped. He dropped the pan and grabbed his heart. I swiped my talons, scoring his face. He howled miserably. I sliced through his neck. His head bounced and rolled into the fire like a devil's snowball. His body slumped over gracefully. I made a decision then not to eat him, sans the head. I had the feeling he would taste bitter. I had a feeling I would choke on his jewelry.

They would migrate to another camp, I knew, Dave needing the presence of other homeless people because he had no wits. I knew they wouldn't move far, being on foot. They belonged no where, and the best they could do would be to move on.

I knew where all the campsites were but I didn't necessarily prey on them--not often, at least. Once in a while I picked someone off who wandered away from the campfire to take a piss, but it was not my favorite hunting.

Midway down Decker Canyon I located them in a camp of day laborers. I curled myself around the base of a rock and I listened to their conversation.

"Comprende! Comprende!" Ivory was shouting at a young man who stirred up the coals in the fire. He wore snake skin boots and a white cowboy hat. He wore skin tight jeans. On his back he wore a backpack. He looked up at her and smiled and shrugged. "It was a big ugly thing, with a wide head like a Gila monster, and a snaky tale like a alligator. Comprende? I've seen it twice now. My dad can tell you. Tell him, Dave."

And Dave shrugged and said, "Oh, I don't know, Ivory. Maybe we just imagined the whole thing."

"Oh, damn it, Dave!"

Dave hugged himself. "Maybe it was just some guy in a monster suit."

"Dave! Come one!" She threw a stick she was carrying at Dave and it bounced off his arm. He picked it up and broke it into little pieces. He grinned and stared into the fire, tossing the pieces of the stick in one by one.

Ivory moved from person to person, one man after another, telling her story, but none of them spoke English, although they listened to her politely.

She had her cross bow with her. She practiced shooting forks and knifes. She used a paper plate affixed to a tree for a target. She stuck the paper plate through a dead tree limb. On the target she drew a monster with almond shaped eyes set close together. She drew a snout.

When they were all asleep and shivering on the cold hard ground I slid quadro-pedal into the camp, and I snatched Ivory up in my hands and I ran with her, screaming, back to the lake. I knew that Dave would simply wring his hands and I was too quick for the others to see me.

I dove with Ivory into the lake and through a tunnel to my underwater cave, and then I set her down, dripping wet and sputtering. She stood pressing her back against the wall of the cave and she shivered pathetically. The lace on her cocktail dress quivered. A stream of urine ran down between her legs and puddled on the floor of my cave. There was a dazed look and I knew she was in shock, which is typically what happens to all of my prey and I was disappointed in her common reaction.

Slowly, with a sense of lazy satisfaction, I stretched out across the floor of the cave. It had been an easy catch.

"Relax, I'm not going to eat you," I said. "I have no desire to choke on that frilly little dress of yours."

"What the hell do you want?"

This, I thought, was more like it.

"Well, for one, I'm lonely," I said. "There's not another one like me in all the universe. But I sense that you and I have things in common. You're angry all the time. I find that endearing."

She stood shivering, pretending to be angry when she was in fact afraid for her life. That annoyed me. "Oh, never mind," I said. "I should just eat you instead of wasting my time. Go. Swim back to your spineless father. I don't want you anymore. Go before I change my mind!" I lunged at her and she dove into the water but then she dropped like a stone. She sputtered and swam like a duck with two broken wings. She didn't know how to swim. I was in the terrible position of having to save someone, which I did, biting a piece of her frilly dress between my teeth and swimming with her to the surface. I put her down on the muddy shore and then I plunged back into the water. The whole experience had been a disappointment to me and I thought about hibernating for a while, but then I decided to wait a few minutes, and then to follow her instead, to see what she would do next.

She ran back to the campsite. "Let's Go Dave! We can't stay here! Come one, let's move!" She tugged and yanked and finally got her father to his feet. She pushed him from behind, and then she ran around and dragged him forward by the shirt. He tripped slowly behind her. In this way she got her father to migrate to yet another campsite up on Deer Creek Road, which was another mile or so from the lake.

It is not comforting to be evil all the time. Not for any moral reason. To succumb every day to a voracious appetite--it becomes boring after a while. I needed the girl as my distraction.

I decided one thing stood in my way: Dave. As long as she had him in her life things would go along about the same way everyday. She would spend all of her time and energy taking care of him and that would be that. But if I removed her father, I would have my entertainment, watching her move through her changes. Watching her fill the void in anyway she could.

I found them sitting around in their new camp, which was no camp at all, but just the bottom of a gully and a lot of wet leaves. They were alone, freezing in the cold night air and Ivory tried unsuccessfully to light a fire and then gave it up. They huddled together for body warmth, and they had nothing but one blanket between them. I thought it was interesting that they would lean into each other and wrap their arms around each other when any other time Ivory seemed full of resentment, and Dave had been all about neglect. It was, as I said, fascinating for the moment. But not enough to put me off my plan.

Suddenly I was there, standing bi-pedal in front of them with my talons splayed; my neck ruff sprung open and my eyes burned, staring wide open. She wailed and grabbed her crossbow. She shot at me. The giant fork plucked at my chest and bounced off. I grabbed Dave off the ground in one hand. He cried in a soft, shrill voice, and fell limp. I took him by the throat and shook him and threw him down. That was enough to knock him unconscious. I had nothing against Dave, and no real desire to make it any worse for him. Out of deference to Ivory, who was trying to stab me in the back with her fork, I did not eat him in front of her. I fled with him back to the lake and there I devoured him in three slow bites. He never regained consciousness. Later on, he gave me indigestion.

When I returned to the gully later that same night, I found her huddled into herself, crying and shivering. Every few hours or so anger overtook her and she jumped up with her crossbow. She practiced her aim. The new face on the paper plate she had affixed to a tree had, in addition to the black almond eyes and snout, a crest of spikes. She was getting better at drawing me. She was a miserable shot but she seemed to get better with practice. I saw that she took her knife and sharpened a long stick into a spear. She took the jagged lid of a coffee can and practiced flinging it like a disk. She seemed invigorated, and soon the target became lacerated until it was nothing but a slip of torn paper hanging on the tree.

I went home and waited for her to come after me with her arsenal. But she never came. For days she never came, and I grew slowly disappointed. I went spying from camp to camp and she was not in any of them, but I have super-sonic ears. I listened to the gossip about her and learned that she had been snagged by the Child Welfare Office. The talk in the camps was about a Dr. Sidhu who had adopted Ivory as his foster child. He was well thought of and fiercely handsome, like some TV doctor. He had a dark, perfect face. He was an immigrant from India and a member of an ashram in Malibu. He performed charity operations even for the homeless and he had adopted eleven children as his own. Ivory, however, was still a foster child.

It was not hard finding her. I found Dr. Sidhu's ranch style house in one shot, once I put my mind to it. There was a scent like spoiled milk which was decidedly Ivory. I stretched out across a branch tapping on the window. The long dinner table stretched across the room and the children sat quietly eating, all of them with manners. Two housekeepers rushed around the room serving plates of chicken and string beans.

"Ivory," said Dr. Sidhu. "There is a curfew here. All the children in my house must be home for supper and they must not go carousing late at night. Furthermore, there is no smoking here. None of my children have permission to smoke. If you are given money, it is for your lunch, not a pack of Lucky Strikes. Furthermore, there is no drinking and no drunkenness in this house." He had the immigrants way of talking literally.

"Yes sir," Ivory answered, but the way she hung over her dinner plate and played nervously with her napkin, twisting it into knots and shredding it, made me think she could not so easily change her habits.

"Furthermore, there will be no more stories about this monster. You are using that as an excuse to drink."

"I'm telling you it was real!"

"Now listen, no more monster stories. It is very painful, I'm sure. Your father disappearing in the night. But there is a silver lining to your bad luck. You came to live here, instead of in a homeless camp. But in this house we do not use things as excuses. That is one thing you must not do, now that you are living here."

"I don't want to be here! Send me away and don't come looking for me!"

"Try to fit in, Ivory."

"Oh, Jesus!"

"And the other thing we do not do is swear, at least not in front of the other children. If you must swear, do it privately."

"Christ!"

"Now that is enough. Eat your dinner."

I saw that she hung over her plate of chicken, a fork raised in her hand, and felt paralyzed, not knowing how to breath in a place like this. Which is why I love her so much. She sighed and put her fork down and folded her hands nervously in her lap. Jiggling her leg as if she had to use the bathroom.

When I saw her next she was up at the camp, lying on the ground. She was wearing her school uniform and it was dirty and torn and tight across the breast, a green rayon shift and a dirty white blouse. The collar of her blouse was twisted, half of it tucked inside of her scrawny neck and the other half sticking up, and she had the shirt buttoned in the wrong place so that it bunched up inside her uniform. She was smoking a cigar and playing a game of chess with an elderly man who had lost the use of his legs. He looked ninety years old. He dragged himself around on the ground and his pants were caked with mud. He wore a confederate flag as a bandanna on his head. "Lyle," she called him.

"Your move Lyle. Quit dicking around. I'm getting nauseated, waiting on you."

"Just hold your horses, sister," said Lyle. He became distracted and nervous and then he made a disastrous move, and she captured his queen.

"Ha, ha," she laughed. "You lose. You ain't got the con-centration."

"You cheated," said Lyle.

"You can't cheat in chess."

"You know what I mean!" Lyle tried to stare her down.

"Ha, ha," is all she said, and I saw her collecting some small change off the ground. She picked the silver coins up with the dirt and the twigs and stuffed them in the pocket of her school uniform. The money, I could see, was still dirty as she stuffed it into her pocket. Watching her, I had a terrible desire. It was the first time in my life that I felt conflicted. I would not call it conscience. It was defi-nitely not that, because I have none, am not equipped with one. When your entire life is about devouring your prey, ennui is a terrible problem. I had to resist what seemed most naturally to me, to wait till she was alone and then to snatch her up and eat her. Devouring everything about her. What a fine meal she would make. All her spunk and irascible rage would course through my veins for a glori-ous moment.

Fortunately, about that time she disappeared, and I could not find her at any of the camps, or at Dr. Sidhu's ranch, where I spent days stretched out on a branch tap-ping up against the house, just listening and watching for some sign of her. I learned that she was in jail--or rather a children's home for wayward children. Juvenile detention is what Dr. Sidhu called it. It was not at all plausible for me to go traipsing through the urban landscape of L.A. to find her, as there was no way for me to camouflage myself against bricks and dirty streets, and little to eat besides humans. Although the thought of an entire wing full of delectable children had enticed me, I couldn't risk it. Not that I was worried about being caught. I don't even know if I'm destructible. It was mainly that the absence of nature made it hard for me to move about very gracefully, and I am always concerned with making every stroke, especially the violent ones, weave with grace. Also, I was proud and discreet; not eager to create mass hysteria.

I became rather lazy, waiting for her to return to Dr. Sidhu's house, and I remember that she took me by surprise. I had been sleeping up in the tree when suddenly I heard her voice in the house.

"I promise," she was saying. "Ain't that enough fer ya?

"And we don't say ain't. We use the proper grammar you are learning in school. And no more skipping school, either, Ivory. That I will not tolerate. Now that you are here again you will have to abide by the rules of this house."

"Jesus, lighten up on me, will ya?"

Dr. Sidhu sighed, he slumped, he turned his back on her and walked away, shaking his head.

"Jesus." Ivory threw her bags down hard on the floor.

I watched her sit and pout for a while on her four cornered bed. There was a white canopy over the poles, and a frill along the bottom. In a while she grew busy, pulling things up from under the bed. Some other children walked into the room and asked what she was doing. She showed them a spear, the crossbow, and a coffee can lid. She also had, and it almost frightened me, a thing she had carved from wood which looked like a kriss, a long wavy dagger with a thick black handle.

"I'm going hunting for a monster," she told the children, a girl named Beany and a boy named Toad. Those were their nicknames. Their real names were Bernice and Tod. Dr. Sidhu gave all of his children nick names. All except Ivory. He had tried once, affectionately, to call her "Ivory Snow." But it was terribly awkward, and I could tell that, while he was fond and loving of all of his children, he struggled to even *like* Ivory.

"Can we go monster hunting with you?" asked Beany.

"No. It's dangerous."

"I want to go," said Toad.

"I already toldja! The answer is no. You just be getting in the way!"

"We won't get in the way," said Beany.

"See this here," said Ivory, and she picked up the coffee can lid. "This is what you throw at him, to cut off his head, and this here is a kriss--you plunge it into his heart."

"It's a girl," said Beany.

"What?"

"The monster is a girl," Beany said.

Ivory paused for a moment, looking down at Beany, realizing she was having a moment of genius or telepathy, to understand that the monster, that I, was more akin to the feminine.

"And see this spear?" continued Ivory. "You lodge it right between the eyes. And this crossbow here, it don't work." She threw the thing on her bed. "There, Toad, you can have it. But you can't go hunting with me. It's too dangerous."

Toad picked up the cross bow and put the thing on over his head, thinking that you wear it.

"Why can't we go?" Beany pouted up at her.

"Because!" Ivory yelled. "You'll be eaten alive!" She lunged at them. Beany sat down in the corner and cried. Toad let the cross bow drop to the floor. He stepped out of it and ran from the room.

I slid down out of the tree and made my way home, back to the lake. Knowing that before long I would be seeing her again. I swam to the bottom of the lake and sat in the silt; hibernation helps me gather my strength. It solves the problem of what to eat for a while, but I wake up hungry.

After a month or two I came up and settled myself in the under water cave. Looking around I could feel that she had been there. I had the psychic sense that she had come every day, looking for me. Loaded to the teeth with her homemade weapons. I could picture her, awkwardly teach ing herself how to swim out of desperation, like one surviv ing a ship wreck--thrashing with the kriss locked between her teeth. It was all laughable and entertaining but that kriss bothered me--it was something powerful which she had created from her imagination. Her moment of genius. She could harm me with it. She could find me vulnerable.

All in all, I decided to taunt her anyway. My choices were quite numerous: should I eat Bean and Toad? Should I destroy Dr. Sidhu and throw the whole house into chaos? Should I devour Ivory?

I settled for a lesser evil. I slid quadro-pedal back to the campsite. In time she showed up with her chess board. After a few games Lyle swore and took her chess board and sailed it like a Frisbee. "I ain't never playing chess with you again."

Ivory laughed and fell back on the ground, laughing up at the sky. She dressed in her school uniform. The hem was unraveling and the pockets were pulled inside out.

"Fetch me something to eat, Lyle. That was the bargain. You lose, you fetch me something to eat."

"Just hold on!" Lyle dragged himself along the ground like a seal trying to reach the water. His useless legs made a trail behind him. He picked up a can of pork and beans. He took a pan and made towards the fire. "That's all you're getting," he said and he showed her the can. He opened the can and poured the beans in it. He stirred the beans three times with a stick from the ground, then he slid over and handed her the pot and the stick he used to stir them. "That's all your gettin," he said again.

She used the stick to eat the beans. "Cold!" she said.

"That's right. That's what you deserve!" said Lyle.

It was at that moment that I sprang on him. All through the camp people squealed and fled through the bushes. None looked back. Lyle tried to slither away using his fore-arms. I was hungry, having just slipped out of hibernation, but I would not eat old muddy Lyle full of piss and vinegar. I jumped on top of Lyle, and then I took him around the throat and I lifted him off the ground. I could have eaten him in three bites but, as I mentioned, I was only taunting her.

She came at me with her spear, poking me hard. It tickled me. I laughed as I dragged Lyle over the ground, off toward the bushes. She threw the spear after me and it

lodged in my left thigh. Hurting me just a little, so that I felt
my leg tighten up. With my free hand I pulled the spear out
of my leg and grasped it in my hand. I plunged it right
through the middle of Lyle, pegging him to a tree. Laughing
uncontrollably, I fled back to the lake as I listened to her
wailing behind me for her dying friend, crucified to the
tree.

Back at the lake I feasted on a dozen ducks and twenty
frogs and a deer. Afterwards I was still hungry, and I had
to admit to myself that I was depleting the food source. I
thought of Dr. Sidhu's house, a seemingly endless source
of small helpless children I could pick off on their way to
school. Devouring two at a time. And I had to admit that
my desire to devour Ivory was stronger. An urge I had to
fight. How empty my life would be without her. Outside of
stalking and devouring my easy prey, she was my only entertainment. I had to fight the urge every minute, and every minute it grew stronger. There was always the sense
that she would make the tastiest meal of all. That I would
be devouring all of her spunk and creativity in a few quick
bites. I was enormously conflicted. I thought only of myself; what would be better, the slow witness of her person-
ality unfolding? Or the quickness and ruthlessness with
which I would devour her. I decided to test her with more
frustration, to see what it was I really wanted from Ivory.

After Lyle died she returned to Dr. Sidhu's house. I hid
myself in the crook of a Eucalyptus tree and stretched out
over the branch tapping up against the house. My hide took
on the smooth dappled look of the bark. I peered in through

the window. It was an odd thing to see, Ivory reduced to a sniveling child. I was disappointed. She sat in Dr. Sidhu's lap and leaned her head against his shoulder. There was terrible resignation in her face. Dr. Sidhu stroked his hand over her hair. The eleven other small children milled about, some of them tugging on Dr. Sidhu's shirt, some of them fighting and bickering, some lost in their games on the floor. Some sat catatonic in the corner, breathing a hard sigh now and then.

"Now Ivory," said the good doctor, "How can I help you if you will not tell me what is bothering you."

"I told ja," she said forcefully, her face distorted with agony, but she kept her head pushed into his shoulder for support. She wiped her tears, and then she wiped her nose with the back of her hand.

"Stop that!" said Dr. Sidhu. "Here, use a tissue."

She ignored him, wiping her hands off on her school uniform.

"Stop that! Here, now. Explain it to me again. Maybe I did not hear you right."

"It's a big ugly monster, a lizard-thing, like I been telling you all along. It killed my father, it killed my friend Lyle, and next it's gonna kill me. It's gonna eat me alive!"

He stroked the top of her head, his big handsome face resting just above hers. She pushed her head into his chin and made it difficult for him to breath. The contrast of their skin color was shocking--Dr. Sidhu so black he was almost indigo, and Ivory so pale white her skin was luminescent over the veins in her neck and her forehead. "I do not blame you for coming up with that story. Your father walking off, just abandoning you in the woods."

"I told ja!" she yelled, but at the same time she held his large hand tightly with both of her hands, and she twined her legs around his. "It was a green ugly monster. It could slice you open in a second. It devours you like a snake."

"All right Ivory. We do not need to discuss it again. If you say it is a monster, than this is what it is, a monster."

And then she burst out wailing. She wriggled and kicked and slid out of his arms. She ran out the door and I followed her.

She hiked back through Decker Canyon and landed at the creek bed, where she found the remnants of a camp. There was a thick bamboo grove, the shoots so close together that it stood, an impenetrable block. Someone had carved right through the center of it to make a cave, and I thought it was very interesting. I didn't believe I could resist the urge to sit in such an unconventional cave. Skin magazines lay about, muddy clothes hung over branches to dry, and there was a dampened fire pit. She crouched down inside the bamboo cave, hugging her knees and rocking. I slid quadro-pedal into the cave, and she gasped and fell back. She picked up a can and threw it at my head as she tried to edge her way towards the entrance of the cave, but I swooped in, laughing, and I pinned her down to the floor. She turned her head away, as if my breath, hanging over her face, was intolerable, and I have no reason to suspect it wasn't.

"What do you want? You here to eat me? Go ahead, I'll go down like a spike in your heart."

"And just how will you do that."

"You ain't gotta worry about it," is all she said.

"Don't worry," I said. "I'm not here to eat you. Not to-day, anyway. I just came to tell you I'm going into hiber-nation.

I let her go, feeling satisfied for some reason. I slid out of the bamboo cave, and I glanced back once over my shoulder to see that she sat up dazed.

I slid back to the lake and sunk into the silt to dream one continuous dream for several years.

When I woke up again I was hungry. I broke my long fast by eating seven ducks and a fox and a litter of coyotes. Then I went to look for Ivory.

I went to her school. I slipped in through cracks in the foundation and into the boiler room and through the spa-ces between the walls to get to her classroom, where I spied on her through a chink. It took me a few minutes to see that she was not a popular student. She was the class buf-foon, based on the fact that she could not concentrate for five minutes. In class she had a kind of minus comprehen-sion of anything that was said to her by her teachers. Out-side of class, behind the girl's locker room in a grove of trees, she smoked weed and drank Ripple Wine.

I began to question, for the first time, my attraction to her. As an animal I had no remorse about satisfying sexual desires--like the ducks on the lake who rape each other. I won't lie. I'm not human enough to lie to myself, and you can trust me when I say I was not interested sexually in Ivory, great beauty that she was.

Toad and Beany were gone—I did wake up *once* in several years, with a voracious appetite.

Never the less, for some reason unknown to me, I woke from my hibernation with a longing more than ever to con nect with someone. And Ivory, in my saurian life, was the only one for me. I had to admit to an obsession over her; my emotions were becoming human. Something like kind ness was emerging, a wish to see her happy. This was known to me as a terrible paradox. What would make her happiest of all was if she never had to see me again, or bet ter yet, if she could plunge one of her homemade weapons into my arteries and finish me off—I decided then to come up with a better strategy for winning her friendship and trust, if not her adoration.

It was at this point that I molted, a painful process which I can only describe as an involuntary gesture of turning one's self inside out. Imagine the pain of having your skin peeled back at a minuscule speed. When I emerged from my tubular skin I glanced at myself in the lake. To my shock I was human. I still had gills, and my crest of spikes had shrunk to a row of nubs. I had curvature of the spine. I found by combing my hair forward I could cover the gills in my neck, and the only thing which would be difficult to ex plain, I realized, was my weave of black and green hair like long strands of sea grass. I developed embarrassment and I had to find clothes to cover myself—but that was the easy part. There were things I had regurgitated up at the lake

31

when I devoured my victims. Things I could not digest. Purses and high-heel shoes and dresses. The one thing which had not changed was my obsession with Ivory.

The thought of victimizing someone seemed remote and impossible to me. All that had changed with the molting. I taught myself to read newspapers and magazines on recycling day, and from there it was easy enough to go to the library and educate myself. All with the intention of fomenting a better relationship with Ivory. I did enough reading to understand how to fabricate a teaching credential, letters of recommendation, and transcripts. I graduated myself from UCLA, Magna Cum Laude.

I took a position as principal of her high school, and I taught an honors class in mythology. The standard joke at this school was that I looked like one of the mythological creatures I was so fond of drawing on the blackboard. Recruiting Ivory for my class was difficult as she did most of her course work in special classes for slow students. When at last I had her in my class, she often sat and cried because the material was too hard.

"How'm I supposed to know the difference between a chupacabra and a griffin and a gargoyle. Don't even ask me that. I'll just get it wrong!" She took her test paper and tore it up and threw the pieces on the floor. I had to acknowledge that for her, preternatural beings was probably a touchy subject. She also cried because other children picked on her.

Foremost was Isabel Loomus, the prominent lawyer's daughter, who held pool parties every Friday night to which Ivory was never invited. Isabel Loomus sat in my class wearing purple lipstick and snapping her gum. As principle I did not allow either of these, and she was made to wipe off her lipstick and throw out her gum at the start of each classes.

"Ivory," said Isabel Loomus. She sat behind Ivory and whispered in her ear. Still having supersonic hearing, I knew exactly what was being said. "You know Chad Petry. He wants to ask you out. He told me to tell you. He's in love with you. He wants to give you his ring." Isabel Loomus said these things with a sneer and an evil grin. She sat at her desk crossing her knees and bounced her leg nervously, playing with the expensive jewelry on her wrist. "He told me to tell you he's in love with you. He wants to marry you. He wants you to have his baby."

Chad Petry was the most adored boy in school, and Ivory was the most pathetic girl. All of Isabel Loomus' friends teased her about Chad Petry. "He told me he's dying to kiss you," said Isabel Loomus, snapping a new stick of gum.

By the way Ivory responded to their cruel humor I could see that she actually loved Chad Petry and fantasized about him.

Occasionally things got out of hand. They teased; she jumped out of her seat and fell on them, scratching and biting Isabel Loomus. If she put a scratch on her, then her father the prominent lawyer came to school to discuss the problem with the principal. And I had to defend Ivory and explain why I hadn't expelled her.

Several times in class her kriss had dropped out of her skirt and hit the floor and I had my opportunity then to confiscate it but I never did. I couldn't help feeling there was a magical quality to this homemade weapon. That I had no business touching it, even if it meant someday she would kill me with it. I tried with my psychic sense to zero in on the weapon, where on her person she kept it, but the effort only put me to sleep.

Worse still was the transformation that came over me. I molted again, becoming my old saurian self, only worse, with sharper talons and longer fangs and a neck ruff that sprang open at the slightest provocation, sharp pointy and stiff around my head. I puffed up to twice my size and I grew ravenous. One by one I picked off all the girls who ever offended Ivory; I stalked them on their way home from Isabel Loomus' pool parties. I devoured them one by one like an anaconda. I devoured Isabel Loomus one night, and, being especially hungry, I devoured her father the prominent lawyer as well.

Then I stopped. I shed my skin at will this time, explaining my absence as a fit of amnesia. There was much talk about town of the *serial killer*, and I felt that with my green hair and my indulgence into mythology and my coincidental disappearance for a week they might begin to suspect me. I toyed with planting evidence on Chad Petry. In the end, I let the whole thing die down.

I decided to go into hibernation again. I still had gills and I could breath easy under water. When I woke, I decided, I would be saurian. Being human was never that comfortable. When I emerged Ivory would be older, at least physically a woman—she would have started her menses, and I too, would be something different.

I hadn't meant to sleep so long or to let her go on without interference from me, but when I awoke again and came looking for her, I found that she was Chad Petry's lover.

I came upon them at Dr. Sidhu's house, trying to make love in secret in the pantry. I would say of their love making that it was hot and clumsy and awfully quick. I had the sense that she would do anything for Chad Petry. I had the sense that he was put off by the smell of whisky on her breath and the smoke on her clothing. Chad Petry, I understood, was just getting laid. Ivory was desperate and lonely and in pitiful love with him.

Chad Petry finished and stood up and zipped himself back into his pants.

"Whew! Damn!" He wiped his hands on his pants.

"Let's get out of here before my dad sees us," said Ivory nervously.

"I'm leaving. I'm going home." Chad backed away.

"All right. But next time you have to take a walk with me. You promised me."

Was she that gullible? I shook my big saurian head. Had I missed something? Was she completely dumb? Why was I interested in her? My attraction to Ivory plagued me, as it had all along. I decided to confront her with her pathetic relationship to Chad Petry.

I waited until he had let the door slam and I watched him running out of the drive way, suddenly full of new energy. Then I slid quadro-pedal down the steps and into the pantry, where she sat on the floor crying.

"No wonder you're miserable," I said.

She spun around, looked at me. I saw her hand reaching for the kriss and understood for the first time that she carried it with her everywhere she went for these past few years--except for the times when she slept with Chad Petry. Then the kriss was deposited somewhere else for safe keeping. I imagined the disappointment she must have felt, seeing me and not having it right at hand.

"If you kill him..." She started in a threatening tone, backing herself up against the wall.

"Of course I'm going to kill him. What's he to you? Has he done anything more than torment you? Don't you think I see what's going on?"

"Please," she begged me. "Anyone but him. Why don't you kill Dr. Sidhu?"

I was shocked. I was disillusioned. I was, perhaps, seeing the worst side of her reflected in me. After that I was more determined than ever to devour Chad Petry, perhaps even slowly, and this I told her.

"Kill me, but leave him alone!"

"Oh, you don't mean that."

And for once she agreed with me that she didn't.

I didn't kill Chad Petry. I followed him, came up to him as he was entering his home by the back door. I climbed into a tree for an advantage point as I spied on him in his house. He was a beautiful young man but there was something so unedifying about him that I lost my appetite. When he entered his house he immediately fell into a shouting match with his mother and father. His chores were not done. He hadn't done his homework. He was late for dinner. His parents listed off his offenses as if they were murder and rape. He yelled over the top of their voices. Without looking back at them he stomped into his room and slammed the door. His mother and father both lit ciga rettes and glanced at each other as if they were lost. In my psychic sense I knew that somehow things were related. Chad Petry had argued with his parents for the one hun dredth time and for this reason he would not be going back over to Ivory Sidhu's house ever again to have hot, awkward sex with her in the pantry. I did not need to feast myself on Chad Petry. As long as she obsessed on him it was a good thing for me. She would be too weak to plunge her kriss into my heart.

I can easily identify, after a while, the parts of me that are human. The part that is lulled into a false sense of secu rity, for instance. It had not occurred to me that, while Chad Petry was through with her, she was not through with him, and would throw herself on him every chance she got. It had not occurred to me that she would humiliate herself, literally running after him when he was with his friends.

I crawled quadro-pedal through the tall grass around the track field at Malibu High, coming just close enough to watch her, jogging and puffing to catch up to him and his friends, and I watched the way they all laughed as she ap proached, how the other boys teased Chad and pushed him and whipped him on the head.

"Hi Ivory," a boy named Buster Blair turned around as she approached. I have an unlimited capacity for perception, and I instantly saw who this boy was--a boy who, given the chance to grow, would amount to nothing and who would make leisure the whole point of a life. "Say, Ivory. Is Chad your boyfriend? Or is he just using you to get laid? Can I be your boyfriend, too, Ivory? Come on," he said, and he grabbed the sleeve of her sweater and pulled it. "Let's go over to my house. My parents aren't home. I want to be your boyfriend today."

Ivory yanked her sleeve out of his hand. "I just want to speak to Chad privately for a second."

They hooted and slammed Chad Petry on the back. But Chad Petry refused to speak with her. He refused to look at her. He fell into a trot and ran away from her, quickly followed by his friends, who yelled over their shoulders, "He loves you! He loves you! He loves to fuck you!"

Ivory stopped running. She formed her hands around her mouth and yelled, taking each word slowly, "I... missed... my... period!"

The boys came to a sudden stop, and then they fell into a lazy walk with their arms and legs like rubber, and they pretended to be laughing but were not, in fact, full of good humor anymore, and they looked at Chad as if something very bad had happened to him and not to them. And Chad just shrugged his shoulders and ran off.

I found myself at cross purposes at that moment. Should I follow Ivory, to see what torment she would put herself through? Or should I follow Buster Blair and eat him. Was I hungry or curious? I had nine months in which to study

Ivory in this new phase. I decided to follow Buster, and when he turned off from his friends and started out alone down the road I came out of hiding and I devoured him, and he went down hard and tasted sour, and I was reminded that a good meal is never someone with a lazy disposition. I was reminded that Ivory, with her vulnerable state of mind, would make the best meal of all, especially in her present condition. I was conscious of the fact that nine months from then, she would taste heavenly.

I had to keep my curiosity peeked, or run the risk of devouring her uncontrollably. After I had finished Buster Blair, feeling sustained for many months to come, I slid quadro-pedal back to Dr. Sidhu's house on the palisade looking over the ocean, and I climbed into a tree and stretched myself along a branch tapping against the window of Dr. Sidhu's study, where I knew the serious business of the house was conducted. I waited there a long time. I waited for twelve weeks and finally one day Dr. Sidhu entered his study followed by Ivory. Dr. Sidhu closed the door quietly. He sat down at his desk and held his head in his hands, pulling on his hair. Then he turned to look up at her, standing before his desk. She wore a big overcoat though it was spring. She stood very still and looked at him with sad resignation. He looked at her as if to do so made it painful for him to see, and the anguish which distorted his face made him no less handsome.

"Ivory," Dr. Sidhu leaned back in his swivel chair and stared up at the ceiling. "The housekeeper tells me that she thinks you are pregnant. That you are wearing that heavy overcoat everyday to hide the fact. If this is true, I want you to tell me now." He sat forward and stared at her.

Ivory let the overcoat drop on the floor. Her stomach was swollen under her school uniform. The back of her dress was unbuttoned to make room for her belly.

Dr. Sidhu put his face in his hands and shook his head over and over. He dragged his hands off his face. "None of my children have given me trouble like you have, Ivory. Do you know that?"

"I can't help it," she said.

"Ivory, you are only fourteen years old. You are a baby yourself. How could this happen? Who is the father?"

She grew tight lipped and shook her head and I would have, given the chance, stepped forward with the information, since I thought she looked ridiculous, standing there defending his honor with her belly swollen inside her school uniform.

"All right," said Dr. Sidhu. "This is what we will do, and I cannot think of another way of doing it. You will go away now and have this baby. And the baby will come home with you, only I will adopt him or her. No one will know anything, except that I have adopted a new baby. Then, when you are eighteen, if you show signs of maturity, I will give the baby back. Otherwise the baby stays with me. Now go to your room for the rest of the night, and if you need to keep yourself busy, you may begin packing."

Ivory lowered her head as she turned to go, and that was her only concession to the fact that she might have done something wrong. She went to her room and she did, in fact, begin packing, pausing now and then to gaze at a picture of Chad Petry which she had cut out of the school year book and pasted to her mirror.

I let her go off to her school for unwed mothers, as I needed to put some distance between us, and so I became interested in the "serial killer" who had kidnapped Buster Blair and Virginia Loomis and several other children at Malibu High-school. The "Left-foot Stalker," they called me, because I had the annoying habit of dropping a shoe, usually from the left foot. Having to do with nothing more than the fact that I am left handed myself and attack from the left side, thus knocking them out of a shoe.

The Lost Hills Sheriffs Station was landscaped with lush vegetation. High bushes banked up against the windows and eucalyptus trees swayed in the wind. It was easy for me to slip into the bushes, or to find my place in the crook of a tree. I spied on Detective Ronny Short as he sifted through the shoes.

Detective Ronny Short caught my attention for many reasons. I did not obsess on him, like with Ivory, but he interested me because he was interested in me.

He had a strange look. A skin disease plagued him and it put me off eating him. Suffice it to say he was a very ugly man for many reasons. First being there was no hair on his face—no eyelashes or eye brows--just as if he'd burned them off in an accident. His skin, troubled with psoriasis, was also mottled with red birthmarks, particularly a hand shaped mark which sat on the top of his bald, hairless head, as if someone were perpetually tapping him there to get his attention. He looked short, less than five feet, I would imagine. He wore tight denim pants and a denim jacket and a white shirt with a tie. He wore the same thing every day, and his shirt, impeccably white, only made his stark ugliness more apparent. His ties bore symbols of something, Daffy Duck or golf clubs or hula-dancers. In the absence of Ivory I became interested in him. So interested that I grew too anxious, perched outside his office window in a low branch tapping against the window. I should make myself indispensable to detective Short, I decided, and that is exactly what I did.

The change is very painful, and when I shed my skin that time it felt like a knife scraping me slowly. A sharp, serrated blade. Like a thousand bloody pin pricks. When I was done I was a bloody mess and I washed myself off in the lake. Then I dressed myself up in the clothes of my victims.

This time I willed myself into a masculine form, if somewhat effeminate. Ectomorphic is probably a better word. I entered the Lost Hills Sheriffs Department and asked for Detective Short. My name is Cecil Livingston, I said, and I have been receiving images of the lost children for quite some time, and I think the clues may be of some value to you in your search. You see, I am a psychic, I told them, and I can tell Detective Short where to find the victims of the Left Foot Stalker. They rushed me into an interrogation room, and Detective Short came in, wearing a tie decked with poker symbols.

"So," said Detective Short, "You have information for us. You're a psychic, you say? I have to tell you, I don't believe in that crap." He scratched at a dry patch on his hands.

"You don't have to. Just let me paw over the evidence."

"Why should I let you touch anything?"

"Because you have no where else to go."

"You're my main suspect right now," he said, and he threatened me with a lie detector test, which I refused to take. Monsters never lie.

"Think what you want," I said. "Just show me the evidence and let me solve this case."

So he let me paw over the evidence, which, as I said, consisted of nothing more than a box of shoes, bagged and tagged. Detective Short sat silently watching me, staring at me intensely, as I described for him the lake:

"I see a wall of rushes, and water, a stagnant lake up at the top of a canyon far to the north of here. Half Moon Lake, I believe it's called. I see Isabell Loomis' stockings, tossed out on the shore. I see that this is the place where the victims spent there last waking moments."

Which of course was not true, but it was the place I regurgitated the things which I couldn't digest. "I see a yo-yo buried in the mud. I see school books and CDs and pocket books and fancy phones with pink petal decals on them. If you drag this lake you will find clues from each of the victims."

And having no other place to look, Detective Short followed my lead, and dragged the lake, finding purses, bracelets, book bags, phones and MP3 players. But no bodies.

"You know," said Detective Short when we met again. "Something in my gut tells me not to believe a word you say. You know that, don't you, because you're psychic."

"Don't be jealous of me detective."

"Ha!"

"It comes easy to some. I see what you can't see. I have an eye into the killer."

"I bet you do."

"I suppose you'd like to know what he did with the bodies."

"Tell me about it."

"Incineration," I said. "Total annihilation. There's nothing left to them."

"And the killer?"

"Self emulation. He had doused himself with gasoline and set himself on fire on a pile of rubbish. There's nothing left of him, either. He'll never offend anyone again," I lied. But I was bored with searching for myself and providing clues to the whereabouts of my victims. I wanted some real detective work to do.

I seem to get my way in things, and though Detective Short never quite trusted me, always half suspected me, yet his superiors were impressed. They gave me an office in a broom closet and a cabinet full of unsolved cases. My job, for the six month stint (all the department could afford to pay a psychic) was to read over the files and come up with leads. I found there were limits to my psychic ability, that most of the trails had gone cold. Out of thirty unsolved cases I only solved three.

The first was the disappearance of a toddler named Emmy Lu, a Eurasian child who disappeared from her nanny at the park. The nanny had stepped two feet away, bent over a water fountain to take a drink, and when she turned back around the child was gone.

I sifted through a few of her personal articles, pawing over them with my hands. A baby blanket she had been overly attached to. The bike with training wheels she had been riding when she disappeared. Her favorite cup.

"I'm getting an image of a truck driver," I told Detective Short. "He is a relative of the family. No, not of the Lu family. Of the nannies. A third cousin. He's your perpetrator. He lives in the back of his truck and there you will find Emmy Lu's downy jacket."

I found myself having flashes of compassion. Real regret for the closeness with which I placed myself next to the killer to recognize him and discover his lair. True, I eat people, but I have a way of devouring them so fast they hardly know what has happened to them. They are horrified and stunned and then I excrete a numbing fluid through my incisors. And that's the end of it.

"He stalked her for months and then he swept her off her bike. He kept his hand over her mouth. She was too shocked to struggle. He threw her in the back of his truck and sped away." I cleared my throat. "Afterwards," I said, he smothered her with his big hand. It was easy for him to kill her, I can tell you that." It was hard for me to tell the truth. They asked me if she had been sexual assaulted. I shook my head and wouldn't go into it. I may be unconscionable but I'm not slime.

John Dempsy, the nanny's third cousin, was apprehended on the highway to Phoenix in a six wheel rig with a load of children's furniture. In the back of his truck was

Emmy's downy jacket. He confessed moments after they stopped him.

I received a commendation from the Lost Hills Policed Dept. for my help. And Detective Short became even more conflicted, frustrated and just plain mad at the sight of me, knowing I had helped solve a difficult case, and yet know - ing in his heart that I was the Left Foot Stalker. In fact he developed a nervous habit, scratching at his psoriasis in my presence. His neck was covered by a dry red patch and when he scratched it bled. At times I offered him my hand kerchief but he dismissed me with an angry wave of his hand.

The next case involved a young intern, Dr. Shawn, who did not show up one day for his rounds, and no one ever saw him again. He left his apartment in shambles—an im- peccable man. The refrigerator had been pulled out from the wall as if, said Detective Short, someone had tried to hide behind it. Detective Short had been assigned by the chief of police to work with me on the case, providing me with any clues which might be meaningful. He did so re - luctantly.

Was he known to pick up women? I ask Detective Short. No, was his answer. He trusted few people, he said, and least of all strangers. But I had to break it to him, knowing it would distress him to be so wrong. But the fact remained that he trusted prostitutes, and one of them had gotten at- tached to him, wanted to marry him, and finally defeated by his total rejection, she had pulled the refrigerator out and hid behind it one night after he dismissed her, and in the middle of the night she surprised him, took a gun from her purse and forced him into his car. She took him for a drive into the Mojave dessert, shot him, and left him wounded, a target for coyotes. Then she returned to his apartment and ransacked the place, looking for anything of value which she could pawn. But he was frugal, and there had been nothing much to steal. Some old video equipment. A wide screen TV which was too big to carry out the door. He had spent the money he made as an intern on whores to abate a furious sex addiction. Finding nothing of value, feeling frustrated that her meal ticket had vanished, she turned her rage on the apartment and trashed it, turning furniture upside down and tearing the curtains from their rods. Only one neighbor remembered a ruckus in the middle of the night.

"And the prostitute, Roxy McDow, can be found hanging out at a shooting gallery on Martin Luther King Drive. You'll find her trophies stashed in her purse—a surgical mask and some other things I can't quite see."

And Detective Short did go to every shooing gallery on Martin Luther King Drive, as he was beginning to realize that I was indispensable, until he found Roxy McDow trying to drown out her sorrows and her love for the young intern she had killed. And searching her purse he found her trophies—a check book belonging to the Dr., a hanky embroidered with his initials, and the surgical mask. Roxy McDow led the police to the place where she had shot her lover and left him to die, and they found his bones scattered about.

The third case involved a hermaphrodite named Sam. He/she was in the middle of a sex change operation. Sam had breasts and soft skin and a high voice but her penis had not been surgically removed, and she had facial hair, a rough beard under her double chin. She danced and sang at a gay club called the Lighthouse on Sunset Boulevard. She was punctual and dependable, waiting tables in between her performances which did not make enough money to survive. But one day she didn't show up. Her roommate, an amateur boxer named Clem, said she never returned and that was suspicious because she had been punctilious about always telling Clem when she would be gone and when she would be returning to their apartment, in the event that Clem decided to entertain some woman while Sam was gone.

But this time she didn't return when she said she would and Clem called the police immediately, knowing something was wrong. But the police waited three days before treating the case as a missing person, and by then the trail was cold. In fact, no one from The Lighthouse could remember seeing her with anyone new, and her neighbors had nothing to report, and her friends all knew her as someone who did not date strangers. She was, in fact, in love with Clem and keeping herself for him. The sex operation was a desperate ploy to interest him in her, and Clem had promised he would sleep with her when the process was complete. The last anyone knew of her, she'd been headed for the Doctor's office, to take another injection of hormones, but she never arrived.

I sought out Clem and asked him if I could sift through Sam's things, to get an impression of her. He obliged me but he was nervous. That was my first clue that Clem was involved, and Detective Short also had his suspicions because of the scattered way in which Clem responded to their inquiries. Thus, as I sifted through Sam's clothes and her shoes, I also grazed my hands over things belonging to Clem, his weights, his guitar case, and his colognes lined up perfectly in the bathroom. I received horrible flashes of Clem with a hack saw, making a bloody mess as he cut Sam up in the bathtub, cutting her into little pieces and stuffing her into blocks of cement. Out in the garage I walked over to Clem's tool box and hefted it. Tools were arranged neatly on a row of hooks on the wall but one hook was empty. I touched the place where the hacksaw should have been, and saw in my mind what had happened. Clem loaded the blocks of cement into the back of his truck, blocks of cement encased with body parts. He pulled a boat and drove out to the Oxnard Marina. Five miles off the shore, he dropped the cement blocks overboard, and wiped his brow with relief. "You have the how but the question is why," said Detective Short, warming up to me a little. "If you can tell me that I'll believe you're a psychic."

I explained it to Detective Short to the best of my understanding--from my limited grasp of human behavior: "Clem was a man of his word. And he had given his word to Sam that he would sleep with her promptly, once the operation turned her into a full fledged woman. But Clem developed fits of agony. The thought of sleeping with Sam pushed him over the edge, and he killed her in her bed one night, forcing a plastic baggy over her head. Killing her had been easier than going back on in his word."

Thus, having worked for six months while waiting for

Ivory to come to term with her baby, I ended my career as a psychic detective and disappeared myself, leaving Detective Short with yet another missing person and an unsolved case.

I was more comfortable as a monster, and for once making the transformation was easy, like slipping into a warm pool of water, or feeling a hot breeze swarming around your head. It felt natural. The wind blew all over me, touching every part of me, and I swam deep in the water, digging my nose into the silt.

Something about Ivory brings out the beast in me. I feel that I grow hideous just looking at her, spying on her. Scales grow over my eyes and my tail curls underneath me. My neck ruff springs open around my head, sharp edged and pointy. I slither into the lake and wait for her to make an appearance, and when she doesn't come, as I expect her to, I grow lonely. Then I slither out of the water and go spying. I climb a eucalyptus tree and hang out over the branch, taking on the smooth dappled look of the mottled bark. To camouflage myself as something is to feel it in essence, so that when I take on the look of the bark, there is also the sensation of being pulpy and wooden and flaky. I could feel every insect crawling in and around me. I lay still as wood and peered in through the window of Dr. Sidhu's house.

Ivory was home from the hospital and brought with her the baby which the housekeeper immediately took from her hands, shoving her away. The housekeeper's name was Billie. She was built tall like a man with big bones and she limped, having a club foot.

"You leave this baby to me now, Ivory. That is the way Dr. Sidhu wants it. You go up to your room now and wait until we call you for dinner. Go to your room and think about how you are going to do better in school this year."

They (Dr. Sidhu and the housekeeper Billie) would not let her mother the baby, and though I felt somewhat uncomfortable perched in a eucalyptus tree to spy on them for days, still it was fascinating to watch this drama unfold. In my human persona I heard once that there was a particular drama on TV, an experiment, whereby a camera was set up to film everything a family did in there day to day events—their anxiety attacks, the arguments, the infrequent moments of soft love. It was broadcast and the whole world watched this one particular family go through their machinations, and sitting, watching Dr. Sidhu and his family through the windows was like that for me. In addition I learned everything about being human. I learned that it takes real nerve each day to hobble out of bed with a face puffy with sleep, hair matted into funny shapes. Ivory, when she returned with her baby, hardly had the nerve to crawl out of bed. While the other children were jumping up and scurrying about to make time for breakfast, she lay in bed and pulled the covers over her face. If the baby cried at this time she stuffed her head in the pillow and folded it over her ears. Then Dr. Sidhu rushed in and pulled her out of bed.

"Come on, Ivory. Do not be a lazy bum."

He threw her blankets off. She threw her hands up to

her face, blocking out the light. He latched on to her arm and pulled, as if he could drag her out of bed, but she held onto the bed post, so that as he pulled he yanked the bed across the floor; the canopy shivered. Ivory lay perfectly still like a magnet stuck on steel.

"Come on. Do not make me angry. You know that you have to go every day, without exception, Ivory. We do not know when you are sick and when you are faking any-more."

He pried her hands loose from the post of the bed. He pulled her up into a sitting position.

"I'm sick. Can't you see that?"

She fell back and covered her face with the blanket.

"Come on. You cannot be sick everyday."

Dr. Sidhu yanked her forcefully, until she was sitting up again. Slowly she moved, placing one foot after the other on the floor. Her face looked scrambled with worry.

This was their daily routine. Once she explained, "They're just gonna make fun of me. They all know."

"You are a Sidhu now," said the Doctor. "You hold your head up high no matter what you have done. Anyway, how would any of them know?"

"They guessed it."

That day I followed her to school, feeling righteous, for some reason. I slithered through the grass and kept myself camouflaged against the outcroppings of rocks with their rust colored lichens. When I reached the school I crawled up an oak tree and lay myself on a branch, flicking my long tongue quickly at flies and ants and tree toads.

When Ivory walked into the class, Chad Petry turned

red, then white. Someone bumped him, a boy named Arthur Droan.

"There she is," said Arthur.

"So what." Chad Petry laughed like he was embarrassed and opened his book, pretending to read.

"Mommy! Mommy!" cried a girl named Sarah Long. "Come pick me up, Mommy!"

"Hi Mommy!" Called Arthur. "Hey what did you name it. Chad? Did you name it Chad?"

"No, stupid." Sarah Long seemed annoyed at boys in general. "It's a girl. Didn't you hear?"

"What's the girl's version of Chad?"

"Oh, shut up," said Ivory.

"What'd you name it?" Sarah Long turned around in her seat, facing Ivory.

"I didn't have no baby," said Ivory. "My father adopted a new baby girl. What's it to you."

"It's a girl! It's a girl!" shouted Arthur.

"What's her name," said Sarah. They both sat in their desks sideways, looking at Ivory.

"Will she have a weird name like you do?" Arthur threw a wad of paper at her.

"Shut up, Arthur," said Sarah Long.

"What? I want to know what her name is?"

"The baby's name is Chantel," said Ivory.

"Who named her *that*," said Sarah Long. And she laughed in a mean way.

"I named her myself."

"Oh, see! See! She's the mother."

"Shut up, Arthur," said Sarah Long.

"Nobody asked your opinion," said Arthur.

Now it occurred to me that I was getting hungry. If I devoured Sarah, I eliminated a potential advocate for Ivory. If I devoured the baby I would still be hungry. And I might even feel ashamed of myself. But If I devoured Arthur I would more than likely get indigestion from his cocky nature. And if I devoured Ivory I would suffer boredom and a loneliness which was horrible.

The problem was solved for me when Mrs. Pierce, their teacher, came up behind Arthur and smacked him on the back of his head with her ruler.

"Turn around in your seat," she said. "And don't let me catch you grinning."

Mrs. Pierce was wide around the hips like a pin ball. She dressed in drab clothing. A pant suit and a brown furry sweater which looked like bear skin. She wore nylons and sandals. She wore eyeglasses on a red string around her neck.

I waited till the halls of school were empty and then I slithered into her classroom, banking up against the wall. I slithered soundlessly behind her seat, and then I waited there quietly until, startled, she turned around to see me. She rocked backward in her swivel chair. Her mouth described a big O as she screamed silently, her head shivering. Her sandal flew off her left foot as I lunged. I pounced on her and devoured her in three bites. She tasted like chalk and her furry brown sweater tickled my throat. I left her sandal under the desk. My trademark. It was Friday, and no one found her missing until Monday when she did not appear for school.

It occurred to me I had two choices. I could manifest into a human again, and take over the job of teacher, or I could sit back and devour each replacement considering it to be a steady food supply. I couldn't for the life of me figure out how to do both.

And both is what I wanted. Never tell a monster she can't. It drives her into a rage. I took my anxiety out on the children, frightening them in their sleep, so that when they complained about a monster in their bedroom at night they were said to be regressing. But it gave me a thrill to come upon Chad Petry as he was kneeling down at his bed to say his prayers, or Sarah Long as she flossed her teeth, or Arthur as he fed his pet goldfish. I gave each of them a fright by slithering across their windows, staring at them with my forked tongue snapping between my per- petual serpentine grin. I knew they would remain fright- ened of me for the rest of their lives—and frightened of be- ing alone. Thus having devoured their peace and serenity, I focused on a human transformation and I sought the job as Ivory's new seventh grade teacher, not taking no for an answer from the principal, Mrs. Grady, who looked like a boxer turtle with huge shoulders and a head which bobbed between them and a long neck. Something seemed wrong with her nervous system as her head bobbed continuously. I had the feeling she would taste like turtle soup. I lusted after her job, sitting all day long in a lazy position and barking orders at the other teachers. I felt that I would like to resurrect my old class in mythology.

As a seventh grade teacher I was a miserable failure. Intimidation kept my classroom in check. Seventh grade bored me as much as it did them, until I threw out all their books one day and started fresh with a new curriculum. When Mrs. Grady complained I devoured her. Although later I worried I'd done irreparable damage to my nervous system.

This new curriculum I devised was called Victim/Victim ization. Each student was asked to draw a picture of how they would like to be martyred. As a direction I showed them a sketch of me, tied to the mask of a ship which was sinking.

Chad Petry drew a picture of himself upside down. His feet were tied to the branch of a tree and his hands were tied behind his back. A snake crawled down his leg towards his head and his mouth was shut with an apple.

"The snake eats the apple," said Chad, "And then crawls down my throat."

"Very Good Chad!" I shrieked.

Sarah Long drew a picture of herself in her underpants being dragged by a horse through a field of glass.

Arthur Droan drew himself in an electric chair. Arthur was criticized by the other students for being unoriginal.

I printed copies of each method of self torture and then I sent them to their parents. I feasted on the trouble I would cause. Trouble is my middle name.

In short time I was arrested for child endangerment and placed in a cell at Sybil Brand Institute for women in downtown Los Angeles, where I met Alicia Wickson, which was all part of my plan.

My plan was to endure prison food and isolation for

about as long as I could stand it and then to molt and slither out between the bars one night and crawl, quadropedal, all the way home, back to the lake. But I had intuited something which Ivory could never know, that Alicia Wick son was her mother, and I had to remain for a while to learn something about her; each day I resisted the urge to transform back to my saurian side and devour Alicia Wickson, thinking that in this way I could become closer to Ivory. A mother replacement, if you will. Perhaps I thought magically. After all, a mother missing is not necessarily a mother lost.

"Got any kids?" was the first thing I asked her, when we sat together in the exercise yard.

"Shit yeah. I got kids, don't ask me where they are.

"What'dya mean?"

"Don't cop an attitude with me. What are you in for, child endangerment. Least I threw my kids away."

"Threw your kids away, did you?"

"I had four kids," she said, sitting on the grass with her weights and staring at her biceps as she pumped steel. Her legs lay stretched out in front of her in a V shape, like fallen trees. Her shaved head reflected a little sunshine. Tattoos of two rearing horses rose up to fight each other on her back. She wore a man's ribbed T-shirt.

"I gave the first one, Ivory, to her father, and told him to take care of her, as I was whoring and shooting crack and couldn't do it myself. He was a loser but he made me a promise, and as far as I know he kept it. My first baby girl. She was beautiful. Born addicted to crack. That's life. Do I feel bad about it? Not really. It was her karma to be born

that way. Just like it's my karma to be doing blow jobs ten times a day to get off. Just like it's your karma to be stuck here listening to me. No place to hide. Listening to me talk about all the children I had and dumped like garbage. Their fathers were all Johns. All except for the one who fathered Ivory. He was just a poor slob who met me when I was striping. I liked him because he bought me roses. Can you imagine? Buying roses for a stripper? He was just a sentimental guy and lonely and pathetic. I felt sorry for him and gave him something for free,
and we had Ivory.

"How do you know?"

"What?"

"If he's the father."

"Who said I knew? I don't know. He was just the poor slob I pinned it on. Who the hell said I knew?"

"So Ivory knows? That he's possibly not the real father?"

"Who knows what she knows? I haven't seen her since she was ten months old. I just now remembered her name. She could be dead for all I know."

"And the father, I mean, the man who thought he was the father?"

"It's the strangest thing." She laughed hard and shook her head, as if enjoying a good joke. "Some homeless guy I know. Says he saw him devoured by a giant lizard. Devoured like a snake. What a way to go." She laughed again, wiping tears out of her eyes.

I grew frustrated with myself. There was no way, it seemed, that I could make her feel shame or guilt about anything. I lost control; I changed back to myself that very night, crawled into her cell and ate her. I think she slept through it.

Then I slid out through the plumbing and into freedom. I tried molting back and failed, do to nervousness I suspect. It was a terrifying night, trying to navigate the city land-scape as a lizard. Almost nothing in nature and no way for me to camouflage myself. More than a few people driving down the highway fast looked and didn't believe their eyes, and I learned I could count on good old fashion human denial. Denial would get me home safely. They would look at me and simply go blank. And I would find my way comfortably back to the lake.

On the bottom of the lake I lay with my nose stuck in the silt and felt an underground spring gurgling over me, singing in a loud hum. I thought about the fact that in my last few human transformations, I had been wicked, where as in others I had been good. It seemed a thing I couldn't count on anymore—my human goodness. After a year of musing over it I rose out of the water and sought nutrition. I was hungry and I nearly depleted the lake. What was left would have to procreate at ten times the normal rate, I re-alized, in order to survive, and I felt slightly bad about it. I devoured the ducks and the opossums and the rats and even the lizards and snakes, although it was like eating my own kind. I went on a feeding frenzy and afterward, I was still hungry for Ivory.

I sought her out by sent and found that she was assisting at a nursing home far inland, directly east of Malibu, where it's hot and cozy. This nursing home sat in a vacant field full of uncut weeds. A cop of trees stood behind the weeds. I had no problem reaching her there, and I wanted to see her in action. My first thought: how would they taste, these old creatures. I intuited that Ivory was there for her school—for some pet project of the new principle's—to reform bad students by giving them community service.

I slimed under the base boards of the nursing home. I could spy on her from below in the crawl space. The nursing home looked like a square brick garage. There were red brick walls on the outside and lime green brick walls on the inside. Chaos ruled the day from a nursing strike, and the old people wandered the halls in a state of panic; they were lost. They couldn't find their rooms. Some sat in wet and shitty diapers. They snagged at people with their strong, boney fingers, asking anyone where their children were, or their wives or husbands.

It occurred to me that I didn't need to hide myself, that I could stand out in the open and pick them off like berries. But I was more interested in watching Ivory navigate this chaos.

"Put your pants back on," she yelled to a man named Smitty, who cruised up and down the hall trying to fondle the old women in their wheelchairs and their walkers. "Smitty, Goddamn it. Knock it off. Put your hands in your pockets and keep them there. Don't touch anything!"

But Smitty touched everyone, grabbing one breast after another as he shuffled down the hall.

"Smitty!" Ivory stood before him. He reached for her

breast. She pinned his arms to his side and picked him up like a wooden sign. She carried him down the hall. She pushed him inside his room.

I had a clear reading that this old man would die soon from exhaustion. But I wanted to devour him whole while he was still licentious and wry, which is what I did, and then I let myself into the hall, slithering along the wall towards Ivory, who marched through the hall escorting people back to their rooms.

I came up behind her. She sensed me and sucked in her breath, pivoting, "You!" She made a grab at her belt and I saw that she felt for the kriss in the elastic of her under-pants. She did the undignified thing of lifting her skirt up right there and plucking out the kriss. For a moment I was terrified. Then I thought fast.

"I'm here to help you," I said.

"You? How can you possibly help me? You're the worst thing in my life!" She lunged at me with the kriss and nearly stabbed me in the neck but I blocked her arm and tossed her in the air, slamming her against the wall. The kriss fell out of her hand and skated across the floor, land-ing at my feet. But I didn't touch it. I don't know why. Psy-chic creature that I am, I don't even know my own mind when it comes to Ivory. Or that kriss.

Then Ivory threw something at my head, a urinal, and I sulked and slithered away, feeling taken for granted, for some reason. I didn't feed anymore that day, having lost my appetite for everyone and everything but Ivory. The older she grew, the more muscular and irascible, the more my appetite increased toward the notion of devouring her and knowing her in essence. I had to force myself into the slower motion of knowing her through exposure, a less exciting but much more lasting effect. At times, it was all I could do to stop myself from devouring her in one bite.

Things I did to keep from eating Ivory:
1. I swam in circles around the lake
2. I hibernated in the silt
3. I ate my fill of baby ducks
4. I meditated.

Nothing worked to appease me or give me relief. I wanted to eat her as much as I wanted to know her. I tried easing into my human nature, thinking that as a human I would feel less temptation. But that was only a temporary solution.

One thing I knew for certain. I wanted to be near her.

I molted again and manifested into a dowdy looking woman with a limp and a clubbed foot and a heavy mustache. Earlier I had devoured a woman just for her dress, a shift with a herringbone pattern. I knocked on the door of Dr. Sidhu's house. I introduced myself to him as a nanny. I presented him with an impressive resume that I had concocted at the library earlier that day. He hired me on the spot to fill a sudden vacancy created when I had devoured Billie.

Inside the house was chaos, created by the absence of Billie. It was noon and none of the children had been fed and toys covered the floor, so that I had to step carefully and even shuffle through a sea of red and yellow plastic.

Several of the children sat on the floor bawling.

"All right children" I addressed them, raising my voice. "Since I am in charge here now we will have no more homework. Everything will be fun and games." And I turned to Ivory as the other children screamed and clapped and hopped on their little legs.

"What do you say to that, Ivory?"

Ivory said she didn't much care, she didn't do homework anyway.

"All right now children. First we will play a game I call blind man's bluff. First you must let me blind fold each of you. Then you must follow the sound of my voice. The first one to touch me is the winner.

"What do we win? What do we win?" All the children chimed in.

"You win fifty dollars."

In short, they were blind folded, and I led them out the door, through the bank of eucalyptus trees to the steep palisade. Each child laughed softly, placing one foot in front of the other. I climbed into a pine tree and hung horizontally, far out over the side of cliff. Below me the rough ocean surf dashed upon the rocks. "Follow my voice!" I called to the children. "Which one of you will be the... *first winner!*" I hadn't thought it out too far except to say that a pile of them, stacked at the bottom of the cliff, would possible incense Ivory, but I hadn't counted on her interfering, which was even better.

"Hold it! Stop right there. Take off yer blindfolds, ya idiots!" Ivory screamed at the small children.

Slowly, blinking, the children looked around at where

they stood at the edge of the precipice.

It was at this point that I lost control. Probably do to human evil, and being conscious of it, I metamorphosed into an abomination, with a human head and lizard body. My neck ruff sprang open and I lay there on the limb of that tree, slimy and pointy and green with the head of an old, pale woman.

Ivory herded the children home. She ran into the house and returned with her cadre of homemade weapons. I saw that the kriss was among them. First she tossed her jagged coffee can lid at my eyes but I swatted it away. She threw a wooden spear at me and it stuck in my left leg, but that is nothing to me, like getting a sliver stuck in your thumb. I pulled it out and threw it off the cliff. Then, I was surprised to see, she pulled a handgun out of her blouse and shot it, falling backwards. The bullet lodged in my back. It itched a little going in and still does to this day. Then, starting towards me, she held the kriss in her hand, and I could see she would plunge it into my heart if she got the chance, and this I could not let her do. This I knew would be the end of me, and there is no after life for monsters such as me, no white light guiding us to calmer waters. There is only now and appeasing appetite. So I slid down the side of the steep cliff and ran away, regretting that to do so would demonstrate vulnerability. And it seemed more than ever that I should have to eat her, not just out of temptation, but to save my own hide.

Thus, having changed back completely, replacing my human head with a big saurian head, I began stalking her, knowing full well that she carried the kriss inside her uniform, tucked into the elastic of her underpants. That she slept with it under her pillow. I felt desperate fear for the first time, knowing how close I was to the end. I tried to manifest into a librarian. Nothing. A mail letter carrier. Nothing again. A priest. Really nothing. I was stuck as myself and Ivory knew where to find me. I thought of leaving here and finding some other stagnant pond to call home. But I loved the lake as much as my life and I couldn't leave it. I loved the lake because of its association with Ivory.

So I stalked her, on her way to school, or the old folks retirement home, or the homeless encampments where she went to play chess. I stayed a safe distance behind her and contemplated just how I could surprise her from behind. Part of me felt ecstatic and relieved, for I would finally get to eat her, knowing finitely what it was to be her. Part of me felt sad, as if I were losing my only friend. Which of course was not true, but then in a way it was.

I spied on her most of all in the homeless camps. That provided me with the most cover, as I sat up in trees or I curled around large boulders and listened in on the conversations that Ivory had with her friends, delighting in her pluck and her irascible nature which I would soon taste in another way.

"Your move," she said to a man named Amos. "Quit dicking around."

"I could take your queen anytime I wanted."

"Do it then."

"No, I'll try to make this game last a little longer."

Amos was a deceitful looking man with wire rim glasses and hair sticking straight up on his head in oily stalks. One could see that everything he said was a lie. Liar Amos was his name around the camp. Sometimes they called him "Liar" for short.

"You're taking too long. You don't have a plan," said Ivory

"Time him! Time him!" somebody yelled from the side-lines. A boy named Baskerville who wore a patch over one of his eyes, though he was not blind in it.

"Make your move," said Ivory.

Amos folded his fingers together and stretched them out, cracking his knuckles. "I played this same moved on Prince Charles over at Buckingham Palace. This is before the fatal accident. Camila Bowles was in a huff because we were ignoring her. The Queen mother receives her just like a daughter, you know. They treated Di like Cinderella till the day she died. Most people don't know that but I do."

"Your move!" shouted Ivory.

"And Elton John wasn't himself at all at the funeral. I asked him myself, John, I said, can you sing, do you want me to sing for you? First he said yes but then he said no. I was going to sing Onward Christian Soldier."

"Move or quit," said Ivory. "Move it, Liar."

"In the interest of sportsmanship, I'll move my queen into a more vulnerable position." And he moved his queen.

"Ha!" Ivory took his queen. "Liar, you are so full of shit it's a pleasure to know you."

"Well, thank you. Thank you very much."

"He's a lying sack of shit," said Baskerville. He wore his

eye-patch up on his forehead.

"Every word I say is true," said Amos.

I listened with interest as I stalled for time, waiting for just the right moment to pounce on her back. I wasn't worried about anyone coming to her defense. I could count on that, I felt certain. I was only worried about the kriss. I could see her hitching her underwear up, adjusting the kriss in her pants as she moved her position on the ground, and she kept one hand touching the handle through her school uniform at all times. Looking at her, hyper-vigilant as she was, I almost felt I had no chance.

Watching the ruthless way she played chess, how quickly she dispensed with her next challenger (Ha! Checkmate! Baskerville, you didn't last five minutes.) I felt perhaps the best thing for me to do would be to hibernate for another year, to come up with a viable solution, possibly in my sleep. One of the many things that Ivory would never mastered was her swimming. She did not have the lungs for it. Or the wings. Not for the deep dive. Or for endurance. Reaching my underwater cave sapped her strength. All of it. In human terms, perhaps, she was a swimmer. But not as I saw it. I felt safest of all at the bottom of Half-Moon Lake, covered in silt, sleeping like a rock.

When I woke one year later, I hurried on my way to Dr. Sidhu's house. I sat up in a tree, a huge winding eucalyptus, and I peered in through the windows. I found Ivory pouring over some large book, a telephone directory, and I saw, as I looked closer with my super-optic eyes, what she'd been reading. A list of lawyers who offered free consultations. I intuited what she was doing: suing Dr. Sidhu to regain the guardianship of her baby. Anyone could have figured that one out.

Dr. Sidhu walked in and they argued, I feared, for perhaps the hundredth time.

"What do you think you are doing?"

"I'm getting a lawyer to fight you. I'm getting my baby back."

"Why? So that you can drag her with you to that homeless camp? Do you really think you are fit to be a mother, with all the whoring and the drinking and the drugging?"

"It's my baby. Who said anything about whoring?"

"I know what goes on up there at those camps. How you pay for your drugs. And now you want to raise a baby in that sick environment. And I will not let you. I will fight to the bitter end. I am the adoptive parent and I have rights. No judge is going to give her to you with your record. Whose money are you using for the lawyer? Mine! Don't you think that is a bit ironic?"

"I earned that money!"

"Doing what? Propositioning my patients?"

"I filed for three boring weeks in that office. You couldn't pay anyone to do it!"

"I paid you to stay in school. I paid you to stay away from Chad Petry. I even paid you to stop stealing my money. None of it did you any good. You took the money and you gambled with it. How you became richer I do not know. I do not want to know. I just want you to leave the baby alone. She thinks I am her father. Why would you want to confuse her?"

"She's mine. You're not the father. Chad's the father."

"Oh, that whimp! The one who runs when he sees you coming. You think if you get the baby back you will get Chad back. Is this what this is about?"

I saw that she stuttered over her words. This is partly what she was thinking. But more than that she wanted the baby. It was part of her and she wanted to reclaim what was hers. I saw that, in her mind, it was like winning at chess and collecting her winnings.

"Just how do you propose to care for this child?"

She remained silent. In her mind she knew she would do exactly as he said. She would strap that baby on her back and flee up to the camps, which has always been home to her.

"It's not your business what I do with her. You're not the father. You're not my father. You're no one." She stood up then and she went into the nursery. When she came out again she had strapped the baby onto her back. She dodged him and he fell over a stuffed chair awkwardly. He turned to watch her flee the house. He sat on his knees in the middle of the floor and shouted at the back of her.

"I am calling the police! I am calling 911!" But he didn't call. And I saw then that he would always spoil Ivory out of guilt, because he did not love her, never did and never would.

Something about their relationship affected me in a way, making me sleepy. Something in the hatred they bore for each other. It made me want to nose myself deep in the silt for twelve years. And that is exactly what I did.

When I woke again, I went looking for Ivory. I searched for her up at the camps, finding her sitting before a camp fire, stirring the coals under an apple she cooked on a stick. Beside her sat the girl, Chantel, sucking her thumb though she was twelve years old. Ivory had a streak of gray hair like a wing on the right side of her head. I could see they had fishing poles and baskets with a few berries and leaves.

I slid through the grass and climbed up an oak tree and came to rest on a branch hanging over their heads. Stretched across the branch I camouflaged myself like the gray dappled bark. I sliced my talons into the bark as the wind blew hard.

"Well," Ivory said after a long silence, "I suppose you hate me now for what I did. Some birthday this has been for you."

The girl took her thumb out of her mouth. "I don't hate you, ma." From the moment those words were spoken I realized that, like Ivory, she was both dumb and a creative genius.

"Wouldn't blame you if you did," Ivory turned her apple on the stick.

"It wasn't that bad," said the girl.

Ivory snorted. "Did he smell bad?"

"Something awful," said the girl, and she resumed sucking her thumb.

"It's our only hope. You know that. You and me sleeping around."

"I know ma," said the girl. "Really, it wasn't too bad. Got twenty bucks. Shit."

"Honey, you're worth a lot more than that. You know that."

I was touched. This, to me and my sick way of seeing things, was a sign of serenity. I wanted nothing more than to slide out of my hiding place and join them around the fire. Well, only one thing more. But I looked first for any sign of the kriss. I saw it, a lump stuck under her belt, beneath her shirt. Yet something told me, my psychic sense, that she was not so eager to kill me now. That she was demoralized by selling her daughter, and too weak to put up a fight.

So I did what I wanted to do. I slid down the tree and crawled quadro-pedal into the campground, and slid over the floor of leaves, hissing forward until I came to rest between the two of them.

"Chantel, move back!" yelled Ivory.

Ivory pulled the kriss out of her belt. She stepped back. But Chantel looked at me and smiled. "Oh! The monster!" she said, just as if she had been waiting for me all of her life. "Pretty ugly ma. Just as you said. Smells bad, too." She stuck her thumb back in her mouth, then she pulled it out again, "We should catch her. Put her in a cage and charge admission, ma. Then I wouldn't have to sleep with nobody."

Ivory sat down on the ground. She sighed a long time. She looked at the kriss in her hand. Then she slipped it into her dirty sock.

"All right," she said to Chantel. "That's what we'll do."

And it amazed me that she could be redirected so easily. "But after we make some money I say we kill her!"

That was more like Ivory.

So I let myself be caught. Ivory threw a blanket over me. I let Chantel take a rope and tie it around my neck and tie me to a tree. When I laugh it sounds like coughing and I coughed almost the whole night, sitting, roped to a tree.

The blanket stayed on my head because, as Chantel said, I was too ugly to look at. I found my obsession for Ivory being misplaced by a longing to know Chantel. I learned that it was youth in general that interested me. Ivory had become old and tired and defeated already at twenty seven. She had bags under her eyes and she walked as with heavy gravity. The kriss hardly worried me. She didn't have the pluck to use it anymore. But this new one, Chantel, worried and delighted me. Ivory went out scrounging for a cage to put me in for display. "Don't take your eyes off her for a minute," she said over her back as she ran off.

Lying roped to the tree with the blanket thrown over my head, I tried to have a conversation with Chantel.

"What's happened to Ivory?" I asked.

"What do you mean?" She slipped the blanket off my head so that she could meet my eyes.

"She's all dragged out," I said.

Chantel didn't answer me.

"Why don't you untie me? I'm no bother to you. It was your mother I wanted, and now that she's old and tired I don't want her anymore."

"My mother's not old. She's just tired, she doesn't sleep so well. We're going to put you in a cage and make some money. "

She stared and sucked her thumb.

I don't mind saying I was lonely. The life of a monster is dull and tiresome. Killing and maiming and eating day in and day out. At the moment I thought I would like to make friends with Ivory and Chantel. I would at least let them put me in their cage, to make some money off me, giving Chantel a break from old men with smelly feet.

Ivory returned dragging a broken refrigerator. She grunted and dragged it through the floor of leaves. She was still incredibly strong. She dragged the refrigerator up beside me. "I found it in the wash," she said, both to Chantel and to me. I enjoyed for the moment being in-cluded in their plans. I saw her thrashing through her pile of belongings which lay in the dirt beside the campfire. She came up with a padlock. She came up with a screw driver and she punched holes in the door for air.

"Get in," she commanded me, sounding exhausted and averting her eyes.

I laughed, coughing and hacking, but then I stood on my hind legs, my feet splayed and my back curved and my neck ruff fanning my head, and I climbed in, trailing the moss and the muck which always clung to my body. She closed the door and I heard the lock click on the handle. I was so cramped inside I could barely breath, which was not a real problem. The sides of the walls were slick with mildew, and the prolonged tightness made me give off an odor which even I found hard to bare. I felt a bump and then I felt myself being dragged along the floor of leaves. I bumped over roots and rocks and ridges in the woods. I could hear their muffled voices, swearing and fighting with each other. After several hours I could hear the traffic on Pacific Coast Highway and I realized they had made it out of the woods, a fete on its own. In my mind I saw what next they would try to do: they would hail a truck down to give them a ride to the center of town, where they would hope to charge admission to a peak at me. Presently I heard some Mexican voices surrounding me, and then I felt my-self being lifted into the bed of a truck. I smelled the diesel from an engine and felt the vibration under me. I could tell with each lurch of the truck where we were at, and I knew when we stopped at Civic Center way, in front of City Hall. I felt myself being dragged again, across the road to the children's playground, which is always crowded during the day. Then I felt myself being dumped on the lawn. I heard the muffled voices of Chantel and Ivory as they yelled out towards the crowd. Chantel was telling people that I would sit up and shake their hands, while Ivory warned people not to get too close. I heard the padlock clicking and then the door opened slowly. Ivory tugged on the rope around my neck, leading me forward. My legs were useless, cramped from sitting so long in the tight space. My smell was gut wrenching. People moved quickly to put their hands up to their faces. I slid out of the box and grinned; I had the best of intentions, of helping them make some money—not to help Ivory with her drug habit but to help Chantel, to give her a better life. But my appetite got the better of me and I threw my ropes off and lunged at the children gathered around. I ate seven children in three minutes. Then I ran off amidst some horrific screams.

I ran up Pacific Coast Highway and ducked into the foothills. Behind me I could hear the sirens from a fleet of cop cars. What did they think they could do to me, I wondered, laughing to myself. How could they possibly think they could kill or capture or even injure me?

Well, I had let myself be seen, and now I would exist as more than just a rumor. The problem of the Left Foot Stalker had been solved, I thought. I sat basking in the lake, waiting for a posse to come after me.

Recycling day is how I learned about the hunting party being formed to track and kill the man eating mountain lion. I liked reading the whole weeks events in one stack of papers on recycling day. For one whole week there were articles about me, only they got it wrong. *Mighty Men of Malibu Seek Murdering Mountain Lion* read the caption from the *L.A. Times.* I wasn't interested so much in the fact that they wanted to kill me. It was more a problem of identity. I felt almost like I wanted to *kill them* for getting it wrong. How could they think for one minute that a lion had done the kinds of things I had done. Were humans really that dull and gullible, even after seeing me with their own eyes? Had I inherited some of this mental midgetry?

The hunters, I knew from reading the article, would meet at Bob Dylan's strange, abandoned, pagoda like ranch which looked more like a sculpture by Lois Nevelson, disassembling itself, then rebuilding itself. It was a structure, not an abode. From the foot of the Canyon they would travel on foot, up to the top of Bony Ridge Mountain, the highest peak of the Santa Monica range which consists of hidden water falls and bottomless pools and petrographs and homeless encampments. I arrived in advance, and thought it best to perch myself in a tree. I looked on from a safe height, spying down with optic magnification at their camp. The hunters sat with their backs to me, peering into the fire which lit up their faces and their great sense of purpose. They shivered and rubbed their hands and smiled in the warmth of the fire. I counted twenty some shapes of various heights and widths, some of them quite round and some even tiny. They wore what I presumed to be hunting clothes. Boxy hats with ear pads. Padded jackets with miss ing sleeves. They looked square in the head, chubby around the middle with thin arms. They bounced in their boots when they stepped around the fire. Some smoked quietly and some scratched themselves all over. Every now and then one would lift up his head and sniff.

"Smell that?"

"What?"

"I didn't smell anything."

"Smells like a swamp. Every time the wind kicks up I can smell it. I don't remember there being any ponds up here."

"Must be water up here somewhere."

"There ain't no water up here!"

"You're imagining things."

"Now I can smell it, too."

"What?"

"I think there's something dead over there in the bushes."

"Must be the mountain lion!"

"She smelled Leon's coffee brewing and she fell over dead."

"Shut up. No one asked you to drink it."

"I didn't drink that shit. "

"Larry drank it. Why do you think he has the shits?"

"Nobody asked him to drink my coffee!"

"Oh, lighten up."

"Something smells back there."

"It's Larry. He's dead."

"Shut up!"

"Take it easy. We'll figure it out in the morning," a large man—the largest of them all—possibly a leader, stood up and stretched. "I'm turning in. You fools can sit here and insult each other all night long for all I care. Just keep it down while I'm sleeping."

This, I felt was my chance, under protection of the dark and before their leader abandoned them for the night. I would let them catch their first glimpse of me. Just a glimpse. I would not try to get too close. I would not overwhelm them with the sight and the smell of me. I slid down from the tree and moved along quadro-pedal, keeping my belly low to the ground, but as I drew closer their dogs snapped off their leashes and ran away howling. Then the hunters began twisting in every direction, lurching for their rifles.

"Don't panic," I called out to them. Confident that my articulate annunciation would disarm them. "Put your guns away. I have something profound to share with you."

"Who's there!"

"Who said that?"

"What the hell is going on?"

Looking up from the ground I could see their faces, all of them perplexed. Some of them plugged their noses and some of them gagged. They all lowered their rifles. This was the first time I realized that my smell was a natural defense.

"Who's out there? Come into the light so we can see you."

"It's against the law to join this hunting party without deputation!" The man named Leo stepped forward and covered his nose with his hand. "Whew! That your horse that smells so bad?"

"I will step forward," I said. "Into the light where you can see me clearly. But first, in the words of your great scholar, *knowledge is virtue,* and wouldn't you agree that the word *evil* is in itself an abstraction of something else, that evil does not stand alone as an *evil thing* but that there is purpose and cause behind the evil, such that if people knew the good they would only choose the good, but know ing only deprivation, they may choose what is evil and think that it is good. Therefore, to know good is to choose it with certainty, and to be less than knowing is chaos. But all that matters, after all, is that we know these things, for in the knowing, we have virtue and are lives, each of us the same, are elevated by the knowledge of the good. For surely, *the unexamined life is not worth living*, as your great scholar has taught you to say.

"What the hell is he talking about?

"Is that a woman's voice?"

"I think he's lying on the ground over there."

"I don't know what kind of double talk you're into Mr., but you better show yourself and you better quit playing these mind games. State your business!"

"I say again," I rose up slowly on two legs, "Knowledge is virtue!" They gasped, they raised their guns, they blasted away. I ran quadro-pedal into the woods, across Bony Ridge, down into Decker Canyon, and I plunked myself into Half-Moon Lake where I sunk to the bottom, nosing myself into the mud. I slept in a hard stupor, bleeding into the water.

When I recovered later that same day I thought about my dismal attempt to be something else, a philosopher, other than my rapacious self, and what a failure I had been. I saw that, as a monster, there was nothing else for me to do but kill and maim. My one attempt had shown me that nothing else would do.

I could hear her from my cave, singing off key loudly and strumming a guitar which was out of tune. Slowly I rose to the surface of the lake. I stood up in the shallows; water and silt and seaweed poured off of my scaly body.

"Chantel," I said. "You can't sing."

"I know."

"Why are you here?"

"I was looking for you," she said.

"Why?" My psychic sense betrayed me. I couldn't read a thing on her mind, and perhaps she wasn't thinking anything.

"My mother talks about you. She talks about you all the time, how she's going to get you, kill you and skin you and stuff you for a trophy."

I liked Chantel. I didn't think I would ever harm her, although I couldn't be too sure. She was the kind of child who talked straight, whose curiosity was her only motive.

"Why don't you swim with me in the lake," I said. "I could use the company. I have been alone for almost five hundred years."

"No. I just came to look at you. I came because she talks about you, how she's going to get you. That's the only reason I'm here.

"You really cannot sing," I said.

"I know that." She slung her guitar over her shoulder and turned to go.

As I have mentioned before, there is no afterlife for me. All I get is what I have, and there is no incentive for being good. Prayer and good intentions are not in my nature. But I kept wishing that they would fall into some money somehow; then they would no longer have to sell themselves for their drugs and their groceries.

Therefore, I decided to rob a bank. I decided on Great Western Savings on a Thursday afternoon. I had learned on recycling days that this Malibu bank, situated north on Pacific Coast Highway, directly across from the lip of the Foothill Mountains, had been robbed four times in the last year and none of the robbers had been caught. The bank was a pushover. How to get myself to the bank without being seen was my biggest problem. I tried molting again; no luck. I decided to crawl down the mountain through the brush, and then to wait until nightfall, which I did. When no traffic was in sight I made my way swiftly across the two lanes of Pacific Coast Highway and crawled over the back of the bank. I slipped through the cracks in the foundation and made myself comfortable inside the crawl space. When morning arrived I slithered along the bank vault. I crawled up to the ceiling. In the morning, when the bank manager arrived I crawled into the seam between the ceiling and the wall and I hung there like a bad patch of mold. I waited for her to open the door. She put a handkerchief to her nose. I saw her wretch a few times. She opened the vault, and I pounced on her and ate her. Thus with the vault door open and my strength renewed, I stuffed a money bag and fled out through the front door as a blur, so fast as to be un-seen. I crossed the highway and disappeared into the brush.

I took my cash and I went looking for Ivory and Chantel. I found them at a campsite. I waited till the dead of night and then I hissed, waking Chantel and Ivory. They woke and rubbed their eyes and stared at me as I threw the bag of cash at them.

"Here. Don't say I never did anything for you. Spend it on groceries. Don't spend it on drugs."

"Shit," said Ivory, and her eyes poured with greed over the money in the bag.

"I told you," said Chantel. "She's nice."

"Don't be fooled. She would eat you in a minute."

"That's not true," I said. Although it was, and then I fled away back to the lake.

Where do I go from here? How do I tell you that, though I had thought the world of her and risked my mortal life for her, Ivory disappointed me. She took the cash and she spent it on drugs. Night after night she got high on crack cocaine and finally heroin. She bought the best that money could buy, and she didn't move out of the campsite. She stayed napping on the floor of that jungle in a state of lazy bliss. Chantel sat beside her doing virtually nothing, sucking her thumb, brushing the flies out of her mother's face.

When I confronted them, Ivory was too shit faced to lift her head off the ground. She drooled and looked at me cross-eyed. I asked Chantel what she did with her part of the money.

"She doesn't give me any of it," said Chantel.

"Why don't you just take it?"

Chantel shrugged like the thought had not occurred to her.

"What are you living on, what do you eat?"

Chantel pulled her thumb out of her mouth. My mother's never hungry. I get a can of soup or I make a big pot of beans."

"Where do you get the money to buy these things?"

"When she's passed out. I steal it from her pocket."

"And where's the money? Has she hidden it?"

Chantel nodded. "She buried in the ground."

With my psychic sense I searched my mind and found where it was hidden, with a dead and twisted northern pine for a marker.

"Would you like me to tell you were it is? You could buy some steaks, some nice warm clothing."

Chantel shook her head. "No. Don't tell me where it is. She wouldn't like it."

She thought for a minute, then she said, "Don't you go dig it up, either," as if she read my mind.

Never tell a monster what she can or cannot do. I went to the marker, the dwarfed northern pine about a quarter mile out from the campsite. I could see that she had covered the place with a bed of pine needles. I dug up the bag of money. I was furious with her for spending it on drugs, and so I took it all, and put in its place a dead squirrel. This, I knew, would result in a confrontation between me and Ivory.

Then, having a patience which is not human, I sat and waited for Ivory, for the expression on her face when she dug with an eager frenzy and came up with the stiff corpse.

Just as I expected, I did not have to wait long. I waited a day, and she came running and panting and jumped down onto her knees and began digging furiously. She wailed and flung the squirrel by the tail.

I slid, quadro-pedal from behind a tree and sat cackling, hissing and swishing my tail. I thought to myself that I didn't know when in the past she had given me such pleasure.

"What did you do with the money?"

"I have it right here." I showed her the bag.

"Give it to me." She lunged for it in my hands

I swatted her across the face, scoring her forehead. It

was not enough to put her off. She fell back and then she lunged forward again. I stood bi-pedal. I took her by the front of her shirt and hefted her off the ground. She swung at me with both arms. I laughed at the comical sight of her, swinging over and over and making contact with air, but I felt incensed as well, and I threw her against a tree, knock-ing her out. When she came to, she lay on her side paint-ing. "Give me the money," she said again.

"I will give Chantel the money, in bits and spurts," I said. "And I will tell her to buy food and clothes with it, and if I see that she doesn't, if I see that she gives the money to you for drugs, you know what will happen. I won't be responsible for one more minute."

Sadly, I looked at her face and saw that she didn't even care about being eaten. She would just as soon I ate her. But she would have her drugs.

"And not just you. I'll devour everyone and everything that matters to you, Dr. Sidhu, Chantel, everyone," I said in a last ditch effort.

But I could see it did not matter either. She lay on her side panting and stared at the bag, trying to figure out how to snatch it.

I lay on the floor of the woods, sad and dejected, thinking that even with all my psychic ability, my strength and my animal prowess, I still could not outsmart Ivory.

I decided to give Chantel the money, and that is exactly what I did. "Spend it any way you want," I told her.

The next time I saw her, she dressed in what looked like a wedding gown and on her feet she wore roller blades. She clomped around on the dirt floor of the camp like a Dutch dancer. Her face was plastered with makeup.

"Chantel," I said. "What are you still doing here? Why don't you get a room to sleep in? Why are you dressed like that?"

"You gave me the money. I bought some things I wanted. And we can't get a room."

"Of course you can get a room. There's plenty of money. Even if you are spending it on wedding dresses and roller skates."

"No, it's not the money. My mother, she can't sleep inside. She says she will never go inside. I don't think I could, either."

That was actually something I understood. I wondered if it was the reason I liked them so much, for, in spite of it all, I was beginning to rekindle my like for Ivory. Not my love or obsession, but a simple like. After kicking the drugs she had gone back to gambling and playing chess tournaments. Fortunately she was a good gambler and she rarely lost money. But she was old and haggard looking now. She had lost her teeth to heroine. She looked like somebody's pathetic grandmother. And she was only twenty seven years old.

My obsession had clearly been replaced by Chantel. I had to admit to myself that it was only the young that entranced me. Possibly because I am so old myself. I am so old I cannot remember being an infant. It seems to me that I sprang full grown from the lake.

Regardless, I had Chantel for my entertainment. And Chantel appeared not to be afraid of me. She wasn't put off by my smell. I dare say she was even curious about me. I hardly needed to go looking for her. She came to me, sat on the shores of the lake and serenaded me with her awful singing.

"Chantel," I rose from the lake with the water and the reeds rushing off my body. "You really cannot sing. Why do you insist on singing if you cannot sing?"

"I'm just trying to annoy you. I'm bored."

"Really!" I was taken by surprise, as always, by Chantel. "Why don't you come in and swim with me. I will teach you how to swim, and then you can come back and visit me any time."

She laughed a mean, haughty laugh, and I saw that I misjudged her. "I didn't say I *liked* you. I just said I liked to bug you, to torture you, you know, drive you crazy. That's why I sing."

I had to admit to myself that I hadn't been very psychic about her, that I had even been vulnerable. I marveled at this new emotion.

"Chantel," I said, "I never really threatened to hurt you. And in all these years I never hurt your mother, although I dreamed of it many times. I always held myself back, and now I am making a promise to you, that I will never hurt you."

Chantel snorted. "A monster's promise."

"True, true," I said. "A monster's promise is not worth anything."

Chantel laughed. Then she walked away, twanging her out of tune guitar and singing a terrible song which, undoubtedly, she had made up herself. A song about fireflies and dragon flies and wasps and bees all descending in a cloud on the top of my head. I watched her go and realized that I was insulted.

I decided to spy on her, watch where she went and what she did. First I had to molt back into my human shape and dress as a social worker. I wore a plaid wool skirt and brown shoes that looked like boxes. I carried a notebook with me. Looking this way I traveled up to the camp and even pretended to trip and screech as I picked my way through the weeds. When I approached the encampment I saw them all, every member of the encampment, staring into the fire pit. Slowly they turned to stare up at me, all but Ivory and Chantel. "Ahem!" I cleared my throat. "I am from Family Social Services and I am here to inquire into the whereabouts of Chantel Sidhu. If you don't surrender her to me I will be forced to return with a sheriff's deputy and take her by force. They all turned on me at once, including Ivory and Chantel, and began throwing things at me. Rocks and burning sticks and empty ketchup bottles, anything which would make a missile. I deflected them with my arms and stepped backwards into the night, laughing all the way home back to the lake. But then I did approach Family Social Services as a concerned citizen and I turned them in. I told them where to find the campsite, and where to find Chantel. I even wrote an anonymous letter to Dr. Sidhu, and I also called the police. I let everyone know where Chantel was. I was thinking if mother split up with daughter I would have my entertainment again, watching Chantel go through her changes. Watching the old fight flare up between Ivory and Dr. Sidhu.

I decided to become an evil social worker for a while; it seemed to me that such a person was part of human mythology, that there was a precedent for someone who was cold and officious and mean. I knew the realty had more to do with social workers who were besieged by too many cases of neglect, but I knew in the minds of people there was a need to establish all fault with the social worker. So I played the part. Creating false credentials was easy to do with word processing and lamination, all things I could do at the local library, which had a nice color printer. I convinced Detective Short that I was from the child welfare office. I came with the sheriff's deputy and I yanked Chantel out of the camp. We drove with her in a squad car, and deposited her at the children's home, for processing, and then in a weeks time we came and got her again, dropping her off at Dr. Sidhu's house. I stepped inside the long ranch style house with Chantel, who swerved away each time that I lightly touched her shoulder.

"Here she is Dr. Sidhu. I'm sorry it took us this long to find her."

"The important thing is that she is here now." Dr. Sidhu tried to take her bags but Chantel yanked them back. "You don't need to touch these," she said. In my psychic sense I was very curious about what she kept in the bag. I zeroed in on them and saw that they carried a rag doll which she still slept with. A warm sweater which was filthy. The wedding dress and the roller skates.

"I'll just see Chantel to her room," I said. "Then I'll leave you two to get reacquainted." I placed my hand on the middle of her back but again she shrugged and wriggled and took my hand and threw it off. Dr. Sidhu tried to hug her but she stepped on his toes purposely. She even shoved him.

Dr. Sidhu tried to recover from his embarrassment. "We are so glad you are back with us, Chantel. We have not seen you since you were a baby. Fourteen years ago. Still, in some ways you look the same. You still have those bright shiny eyes."

"Cut the crap. Where's my room." Chantel tugged on her bags as Dr. Sidhu tried to take them.

"We do not swear in this house," said Dr. Sidhu, "But you will have plenty of time to learn the rules."

"I don't follow rules," said Chantel.

"As I said, you will have plenty of time to learn the rules of the house. Follow me," and Dr. Sidhu turned stiffly and began leading Chantel to her room, which, I noticed, was her mother's old room, with the same canopy and lace cur tains. A dream room for any girl other than Chantel or Ivory.

Now that I had separated mother and child my work as a social worker was over for the time being. The next time I would visit Ivory, I would be my old self again.

I returned to the lake and sank into the water, renewing myself in the slime and the silt and the soft mucky bottom. My transformations were still painful, like pulling skin off from head to toe and turning yourself inside out, but the benefits of being both human and monster outweighed the trouble. I molted again and left the skin hanging from a tree. When I slipped into the water it was with delicious calm and serenity. I was always at my best as a monster.

After sleeping for several months I awoke and ate a school of fish and a family of opossum and somebody's stray dog. I was still hungry, and the dog had whetted my appetite. I knew where four mastiffs were caged up at the top of Decker Canyon, and I went there and feasted on all four. They tried to fight with me, which made the meal all the more delectable, as if I had actually earned it. Thus, feeling full, I went to see Chantel without any worry; I would not succumb to eating her or any other of Dr. Sidhu's children on that day.

I found Chantel in her room, hammering away at a piano which, in my recollection, had never been there before. I assumed that Dr. Sidhu had tried to win her over with it. Again, she could not sing. The music she made was mere cacophony. I slid over the window, looking for a crack in the foundation, and finding one I slid inside and perched myself on the floor at her feet. I hissed, letting her know I was there. She started when she saw me, then she began banging away harder at the keys.

"You can't sing and you can't play," I stated, matter of fact.

"I sound like a frog, don't I," said Chantel.

"Yes you do."

"But if I keep trying, someday, one of these days a song will come out."

"What for?" I asked. For in spite of everything I knew about humans, the answer eluded me; I hissed and I growled and I spoke multiple languages perfectly but I did not sing.

"I'm telling a story," she said. "The story of my mother and the monster."

I was delighted at first. Monsters are self-centered, don't let anyone tell you otherwise, and we delight in the thought of becoming subjects of ballads and books and poems. But my second thought was to worry. Would she describe me as having a beautiful ugliness, which would only be the truth? Or would she miss the mark? Like Ivory, she was none too bright. Did she have the spark of creative genius it would take to tell my horrific story?

"Let me hear it," I said, thinking I was about to be serenaded. Even though she couldn't sing, still I wanted to hear all about myself.

She began by describing my smell, like the bottom of a garbage can. She sang about my nose, pug and twitching. She sang about the way I devoured my prey, like a big mouthed snake. I looked, she said, like an alligator crossed with a chicken. This was not going well at all. I asked her, why couldn't she tell the truth about me?

"This is the truth," she said. "From where I'm sitting."

"Stop this nonsense. Sing another song right this instant!"

So she sang another song, this time describing me as smelling like rotten eggs, and looking like an eagle crossed with a hog.

"Enough!" I swept her off the piano bench with my tail. She fell to the floor laughing. I caught her up in my talons and shook her and threw her down. How did she know I wouldn't eat her? How did she get the better of me? In all my hundreds of years not one living entity had overpowered me and now here this thumb-sucking teenager was getting my goat. How could this happen to me?

I needed to teach her a lesson. Threatening to devour her would put her in pain and teach her a healthy respect for my awful nature. When I told her that was exactly what I intended to do, she leapt up and sat at the piano and began banging on the keys with furious rage. She sang a new ballad made up spontaneously in her head, about my smell again, this time like the stink of a thousand dead skunks, and my look was like a toad crossed with an ostrich. I realized something then. Just as Ivory had her kriss, Chantel had her piano. As long as she played a certain awful way I was powerless to hurt her, and I was powerless to hurt her mother.

It was about this time that Chantel became a petty thief, stealing bicycles and selling them to a fence. None of Dr. Sidhu's children had bicycles any more. She'd spend the money on musical instruments, bongos and marimbas and gongs. She set herself up in Venice as a street musician. What I wouldn't give to see her performance, I thought. So I molted again and for some reason which I attribute to my growing relationship with Chantel, it was more painful than ever, like my hide was being ripped slowly in incremental inches from my skin. I dressed this time as a Venice palm reader. I found her beating her bongos un-rhythmically with her feet and banging senselessly on her marimbas and banging her gong with her elbows. She twanged on her electric guitar with its piggy back amplifier. She wailed on a harmonica, which sounded like brakes screeching. She bellowed out words to a spontaneous song. She was tone deaf, and each note was either sharp or flat. She placed a pick in her mouth and twanged on her guitar with her mouth.

She wore the long wedding dress and the roller skates. Her sign read, "Tell me to shut up. $5.00." She appeared to have a steady stream of customers. She would quit for five minutes, until she was out of earshot of her paying customer. Then she would start up again. Singing in her tone deaf way. I approached her, dressed with a scarf knotted on my head, a flowing silk skirt. My hands were old and veined and spotted. I offered to read her palm in exchange for silence. She struggled out from under the instruments surrounding her and handed her palm over to me. I took her small, smooth paw. I passed my fingers over the lines in her soft skin. "I see that you will have four years of bad luck, followed my four years of good luck. You will marry five times. Don't bet money at cards, you will only loose it. I see a dark, shadowy figure hovering over you. Very sleek and handsome. She has the power to destroy you, or she could help you. Do whatever she tells you to do, or you will be doomed."

Chantel thanked me and said my time was up. If I wanted her to shut up I would have to pay five dollars. And she began banging on her instruments again.

It was at this point, having her dismiss me this way, that I realized I was losing my grip. I would eat her if I didn't watch myself. The cuter she grew, the more I desired to devour her. I thought of Ivory, trying to displace some of my hunger. Couldn't I eat her, and finally satisfy an old craving? I thought it was worth a try, for if I ate Chantel I would have the most delectable meal of all but I would surely miss my entertainment.

I approached Ivory, after molting back, at the bottom of the campsite. Not wanting to create mass hysteria, I waited until she was alone, lying with her head on the ground and her tequila bottle nestled against her breast like a baby. I wondered, for a moment, how the tequila bottle would go down and how I could wrestled it away from her so that I wouldn't have to digest it.

How many times had I wanted to eat her. Looking at her now, I saw that she was pathetic. It took my appetite away. I realized again that it was only young blood that enticed me. If Chantel were to grow old I might lose interest in her, too. I thought of how tasty Virginia Loomis and all of her young friends had been, how her lawyer father had gone down like old leather.

I crept up to Ivory. I slithered through the floor of oak leaves and perched on a rock overlooking her head. "Ivory," I said. "Wake up. I would like you to be awake for this. I am finally here to eat you. I have been waiting for this moment for a long time."

Ivory opened her eyes. She dragged her head up from the floor of the woods. She squint her eyes and toasted me with the tequila bottle.

It was at this point that, psychic creature that I am, I saw that she was only shamming. She was not drunk at all, she had set a trap for me. Her hand moved slowly toward the inside of her shirt where she hid the kriss.

She pulled it out and lunged. "This is for Chantel," she

said, and she stabbed me in the throat. I gasped and fell back and slid out of her view with the kriss still embedded in my neck. I thought I would bleed to death. Because of my psychic sense I had been just ready enough to block her blows, and the kriss had stabbed me but not deep enough to be fatal. I fled back to the lake, where I tugged the kriss and let it drop to a watery grave. I lay on the floor of the lake nursing my wound for a solid month, and when I recovered, I came looking for Ivory.

I found her in the camp, playing poker with faded cards. I didn't even wait. I slid into camp and pounced on her. People ran, "Get out of my way! It's the thing! The thing in the swamp!" They abandoned her. The woods grew instantly quiet except for the wind in the trees. Circling her neck with my claw, I held her off the ground. My stomach growled. We eyed each other, me with a cold stare, and Ivy, with contempt. Her wide open eyes never flinched. I would remember that stare for the rest of my infinity. I devoured her in three slow bites. She tasted like hot butter.

After eating Ivory I developed a digestive problem, a terrible heart burn which made breathing so painful I could barely move. I lay still and took my breaths in shallow gasps and gave up eating anything, so that she nearly finished me without a single stroke. She was killing me. I knew I had to do something to survive. Regurgitating her was too late. I lay around the lake in the sun and it was too painful to move even an inch. In addition to that a terrible depression set in. A sense of disconnection and disillusionment. I had waited all this time to eat her, and now it was over. The euphoria I anticipated, the anxiety of putting it off, none of this existed any more. And I had to admit, I missed Ivory, and I had only myself to blame for the fact that I could never creep up on her again.

Months went by and I had not eaten more than the ants and flies which I flicked with my tongue, and I was growing weaker. I was on my death bed when Chantel came to see me.

She crept up and crouched near my head. "You killed my mother," she said.

In my delirium I looked at her and thought I saw Ivory. "No, no," I said. "Ivory, don't kill me."

"You killed her," she said.

"Ivory, bring me some water."

"Can you bring my mother back? Did you kidnap her? Did you kill and eat her?"

"Ivory," I said. "Help me. Bring me something, a snake. Something small to eat."

And Chantel searched around the lake and found a baby rattler and she fed this to me, and she brought me fetid water from the lake and bathed my head in it. Then she went away.

Thus revived I slid into the water and slipped into a ten week hibernation. When I woke the heartburn was gone. I ate a flock of ducks and a pair of dogs that wandered up to the lake. Then I went looking for Chantel.

I found her at Dr. Sidhu's house. I crept into a tree tapping up against the window and peered into the playroom. Dr. Sidhu stood with his face in his hands and Chantel stood before him. Slowly Dr. Sidhu dragged his hands off his face. Chantel was dressed in the wedding dress, now filthy and ragged and falling down off her shoulders. The train had netted leaves and sticks.

"Chantel," said Dr. Sidhu. "Detective Short was here this morning, to discuss the disappearance of your mother. We have had strange reports from some of the people who live in the camps. You know what people I mean. As best we can figure out, a mountain lion may have attacked her. This is very hard for you to take, I am certain. And it is hard for me to tell you. But several reports indicate that she was mauled by a large animal, and she has not been seen since."

"I miss her," said Chantel. "I miss my mother."

"If I could make it all go away, I would. But unfortunately we have to live in reality.   That is why when you say this monster kidnapped your mother, well, I feel we need to come to terms with what really happened."

"It's ugly, like a Gila monster, with a big fan around its head, and a long pointy tale, and a crest of spikes, and a forked tongue..."

"A mountain lion, Chantel."

"No. It kidnapped my mother, but I don't think it ate her."

"Let's try to live in reality, Chantel."

"Reality." Chantel shook her head like the word was distasteful to her. "My life's got nothing to do with reality. A big ugly monster came and took my mother away and I've got to get her back."

And she turned and started out the door with her wedding train sweeping the floor, catching up toy trucks and puppets.

"Wait! Not so fast!"

Chantel paused at the door but she didn't turn around.

"I want you back here before dark. There is a curfew in this house. You will be expected at dinner time. You will take your place with the other children and you will not be late, is that clear?"

Chantel shrugged. Then she passed out the door.

Dr. Sidhu placed his head in his hands and shook it over and over.

I was pleased by what I saw. The fact that Chantel didn't believe I had eaten her mother surprised and delighted me. I had been worried about losing her. But she couldn't face the obvious. And so her only hope was to imagine that I had a heart, that I had not devoured her mother but was only keeping her hidden in my watery cave. I decided it would be best for me to entertain that thought with Chantel. If she knew the truth, no telling what she would do. I had no idea how she would try to assault me. My psychic sense failed to reveal anything.

I slithered back to my lake and sat basking in the sun, waiting for an appearance from Chantel. I didn't have to wait long.

"Where's my mother?"

"How would I know? I don't keep tabs on her."

"Did you eat her?"

"Of course not. Why would I eat such a polluted, wretched being?"

"Everybody says you did."

"Everybody lies."

"If I find out that you did..."

"What? Will you come after me? How will you do that? I am as strong as ten of you and I can hide out under water. You can't even swim. Like your mother before you, you're just a helpless, spineless human of very little means. You hardly threaten me."

Chantel tore a long blade of grass and stuck it in her mouth, chewing. I could see that she was in no hurry to go anywhere. We fell into a staring contest. After a long pause she said, "Show me where she is then, if you didn't kill her."

"I told you, I have no idea. It's true I thought of eating her but I changed my mind. She ran away. Can you blame her?"

"You better not be lying."

"Idle threats again."

She chewed on her blade of grass. Then she spit it out and began sucking her thumb. She turned to go.

It took all of my courage not to pounce on her from behind. I even thought of kidnapping her and bringing her down to my watery cave. The more I looked at her, the hungrier I got. How could I appease this hunger? If I ate Chantel, after eating Ivory, I would have nothing and no one to spy on. What a drag life would be. So I appeased myself by slipping over to Dr. Sidhu's house and devouring three of the small children when they went out to play in their sand box. It was a dangerous move. Detective Short lead a search party through the Foothill Mountains. They murdered an innocent mother cougar with cubs to feed, but I had talked with her before; she was already stressed to capacity with encroachment. Still, it was traumatic for me to see her hunted down and slaughtered for nothing. I hiked back down to Dr. Sidhu's house for a little stress relief of my own, wondering if I had ever been this rapacious before encroachment.

Detective Short arrived at the house. From the window I saw him talking to Dr. Sidhu. It seemed strange for such a short man to assume a grave look. I pressed my supersonic ear to the wall and made the wind stand down. Detective Short asked to be left alone with Chantel. Dr. Sidhu turned on his heels and walked out of the room with a forward motion. He didn't look back.

Chantel sat down on the floor with the TV remote and began clicking through the channels. Detective Short came and stood in front of the TV. I listened to what he said:

"Chantel, that's a pretty name. Your mother must think you are very special to give you such a pretty name."

Chantel shrugged and clicked the channels, straining her neck and head as she tried to peer around Detective Short to see the TV. After a while she stared at him intensely, as if she could stare through him.

"Tell me about your monster," said Detective Short, peering down at her. "I want to know everything. I won't be condescending. I'll listen and I won't interrupt."

"Condescending," said Chantel, and she laughed.

"It means I won't talk down to you. I'll believe you."

Chantel said she knew what it meant, but in reading her mind I saw that she didn't have the slightest idea.

"How is it that I have never seen the monster?" asked

Detective Short.

"She's smart. She only lets you see her if she wants you to. And then she puts a spell on you, so you can't remember. She's like a witch. She's very powerful. More than a detective."

I was wondering what he thought as he talked to her. I read his mind: he was thinking that she must be an emotional mutant, growing up in the camps the way she did.

"What does this monster look like?"

"She looks like a dragon."

"What do dragons look like? Does she breathe fire?"

"You said you wouldn't do it."

"What?"

"You know, condensation."

"Oh, you mean condescension. All right, let's just say for the sake of argument that there really is a monster. That she is powerful like a witch and breaths fire like a dragon. Where does she live?"

"Up at Half-Moon Lake. She lives in a cave. I think that's where she took my mother."

I saw Detective Short going over in his mind the significance of Half-Moon Lake, the place where I had previously lead them in our search for the Left Foot Stalker. He rubbed his hairless face and then he sat down quietly on the floor next to Chantel, almost folding into her lap as he leaned in close to her. I could see that he was making the connection. That he realized he must pay attention to Chantel. That Ivory must surely be dead.

"When was the last time you saw your mother?"

"She was up at the camp. There was a poker tournament. She won a lot of doe and paid someone to go get her a bottle of tequila. They did and she drank some, falling off to sleep. She fell asleep sitting up against a tree. In the morning, when I woke up, she was gone, but I could see the slither marks in the dirt around the tree. I knew that monster had gotten her. But the monster would not eat my mother, like she does everyone else."

"Why not."

"Because I would kill her."

I gasped, so loud they both turned to stare toward the window.

I receded back into the tree.

"Must be a hawk nearby," said Detective Short.

"That weren't no hawk," said Chantel, and she stared at him.

I retreated in a hurry, stopping just long enough to snatch a few school children on their way home, picking them off one by one so fast they hardly had space to run. I left my trade mark: their left shoes. What Chantel said, about me looking like a dragon, made me think more than ever that I was indestructible, that I had nothing to fear from Detective Short. But what Chantel said made me feel, paradoxically, like a fragile baby, like one who cannot survive without its creature comforts. I wanted to be nursed back to safety and security by Chantel, and here she was talking about killing me. What a dilemma it posed! How important it became to me to preserve the lie that I had not killed Ivory!

Gretchen Van Lente

One day soon, up at the lake, she sat down in the mud, just plunked herself down without a care about getting dirty. Which surprised me because she dressed meticulously in a pinafore like something from the 19th century. I rose up so that only my eyes and nose emerged from the water, moss and silt clinging like a mantel to my head.

"I know," she said.

"Know what," I lifted my lips out of the water.

"That you killed my mother. You ate her. For a long time I pretended that wasn't true. Partly because I liked you. But now I know it has to be true."

"Why does it have to be true?"

"Because she wouldn't leave me."

That made me feel awful, like the heartburn and terrible depression after eating Ivory. Was this part of Chantel's plan to destroy me, to throw me into a depression? Did she know I would suffer remorse? That I was just human enough to feel sorry for myself?

"Well you're wrong," I lied. "I did not eat your mother. Maybe she grew scared and ran away."

"No." Chantel got up." You ate her. You got weak." I watched her back as she walked off, dragging her guitar case.

I resumed spying on her, and I discovered her at the Malibu High Swimming pool, taking beginners swimming lessons. It is difficult to teach young teenagers anything, and that was the case with Chantel. She splashed about and then sunk to the bottom of the Malibu Pool, needing to be rescued by the lifeguards on duty. I wondered why she put

103

herself through the torture. There had to be something more to it than me. It was at this time that I realized I could read little of her mind. She willingly closed it off to me, for some reason. I began to feel defenseless. One day I spied on her in Dr. Sidhu's basement, carving something which looked like a kriss. I loved her dearly but I realized that I must destroy her to save myself.

I began to experience panic attacks, having to do with the fact that Chantel was carving kriss after kriss after kriss, trying to get it right. Trying to perfect her carving, until at last she had a long wavy blade and a sharp point and a thick black handle. I worried about dying, about drying up in a pool of my own blood and becoming nothing so much as fetid matter, decaying and going rotten with stink. Small surprise that I panicked each time I thought of that kriss.

I perched on a branch outside her window, tapping against the glass. "Chantel," I called in a hoarse voice.

I woke her. She came to the window and opened it. I could feel the panic coming on. I didn't know for sure but I assumed she slept with that kriss under her pillow.

"Why do you want to kill me? What have I ever done to you? I thought you liked me. Who will you sing about when I'm gone?"

"You killed my mother," said Chantel. "And now I'm going to kill you, unless you get me first."

"I could pounce on you this minute," I said.

"Then do it. What's stopping you?"

"What's stopping *you*," I said.

And we stared at each other, each one knowing that we couldn't go through with it, at least not yet.

"What's stopping me?" asked Chantel. "What's stopping me is that you gave me all that money. You liked my mother when no one else did, even if you did eat her. What's stopping me is that you're in my songs. I liked you. I liked to torment you. There's a lot that's stopping me. But it won't stop me forever. Someday I'll get over it. I will remember only that you ate my mother like a bitter snake, and in that moment I will forget all the other rea-sons, and plunge my knife into your neck, watching you bleed into the water."

"What's stopping me," I said, since we were playing that game, "Is that I'm lonely. As long as you are in the world, I know that some one person is irascible and stub-born. That means something to me. But it can't last for-ever. Some day in a hungry fit I will devour you for sure." I panicked, even thinking about it. She clearly had the upper hand. Without saying good-bye I turned my back and slith ered out of the tree and I heard her close and lock the window.

I was in turmoil, so panicked I couldn't eat. I was in trouble, starving myself to the brink of death. All because of Chantel. She had strength, I knew, that went far beyond anything that Ivory had possessed. You would not find Chantel touching the liquor. She would not grow old and weak before her time, but instead grow stronger, wiser, and more angry. But could she teach herself to swim? If she caught me napping in my underwater cave, and plunged her kriss into my neck, my life would be over. The Left Foot Stalker would be no more.

It made it difficult for me to sleep. I spied on her at the Malibu pool. I lay low in the grass as she tried to master a class in scuba diving. To my great relief she was awful at it; she splashed around like a bird in a shallow bird bath, unable to even lower her face in the water. Needless to say they flunked her. The sight of that gave me just enough peace of mind to eat and then to sleep. I ate her instructor when he was alone, locking up the pool. And feeling sustained I floated down to my cave and fell into hibernation, thinking that she would never learn to swim. At least not any time soon.

When I woke, several years later, I was surprised at myself. I hadn't meant to sleep so long. I chided myself for being so vulnerable. Then I went looking for Chantel.

I climbed into a tree tapping up against the glass in Dr. Sidhu's study. No sign of Chantel there. I slid in through the cracks and slithered down into the basement. Three years had passed and at first I didn't recognize Chantel--she looked so much like Ivory. For a moment I forgot I had eaten her, and thought she was back. It was a powerful dejavu. Chantel lay on the floor and laying on top of her, kissing and petting her, was a sandy haired boy who looked, in my memory, just like Chad Petry. But it was no dejavu. I waited until their petting was done--they stopped before coitus--and the boy got up and left, just as Chad Petry had once run off. He brushed himself off and ran out the door with renewed energy.

She sat in a daze, listening to the sound of his feet as he pattered away.

"Do you mind telling me who that is?" I slithered out

from behind the water heater.

"What's it to you," she never acted surprised to see me, and she certainly wasn't afraid of me. I incited no fear in Chantel, and I loved her for it.

"It means a lot to me if he is who I think he is."

"What does that mean?"

"That means he's the spit'n image of his father, Chad Petry."

"So."

"So Chad Petry was your father!"

"So."

What was I to do? I was beside myself. How could she be so callous?

"That's incest, you dodo. Do you want to create another monster, another abomination? For all I know that's how I was born."

"So." She walked off, leaving me slithering in circles on the basement floor.

One thing felt definite, as long as she was love sick for her brother, she would not have the energy to come after me. That nightmare dream was on hold, and I could afford to move about, satisfying my appetite with human stock, and a few domestic pets now and then for appetizers. I have learned that there are people so alone in this world that almost no one finds them missing. And when they do no - body cares, and these lonesome types became my next victims. Very easy kills. Not the best eating but still it sustained me.

In the meantime, Chantel continued to see her boyfriend, named, she told me, Brad. Brad Petry. Each time I crept up on her I warned her about the outcome of sleeping with him, but her reaction was always the same. She didn't care. She didn't care about anything. Much like Ivory.

And sure enough she became pregnant. Although she was able to keep it a secret form Dr. Sidhu by wearing a varsity jacket--Brad's, actually. And when it came time to deliver the baby she came, surprisingly, to me.

"Push! Push! Push!" I told her. She wailed and her face became like a prune and she swore and screamed, lying on her back in the shallow end of the lake, so that when the baby came it swam into my hands, and when Chantel looked at it she screamed.

I hope you've learned your lesson, I said, and held the baby up, more mine than hers. A real freak, with webbed hands and toes and a snout and a row of nubs across the head and down the spine to the top of its snaky tail.

"Is it a girl or a boy," she asked

"I don't think it's either," I said.

But I kept the baby. I fed it fish at first, then frogs, and finally one day it was so hungry that I fed it a litter of wild kittens. Every month or so Chantel would ride her bike out to the lake to see how her monster was growing, and I would swim with it up to the surface of the waters and show it to her.

"Good God," she shrieked. "It gets uglier every time."

"But it looks like you," I said because it did, in the eyes.

"It's ugly. Keep it away from me." And Chantel would ride off on her bike, grateful, I suppose, for what I had done for her baby.

Now there were two of us. Two monster mouths to feed.

And though I tried to teach a little monster etiquette this teenage monster was beyond reach. It didn't listen to me. Being hungry all the time, it raped the lake of wildlife with out even thinking about the balance in nature. But it was mine to keep, and I loved it. For once I was not obsessing on Chantel. I had my own child now. Awful as he was, he was mine.

And I did determine it was a he. It was not easy. Finally it was the way he lacked certain grace. When he killed it was never for sport. The violence had no chorography to it. He killed at a lunge, for appetite only, and this lead me to declare him a male. If he had been a female like myself, a sense of grace would also be necessary for sustainability. Male monsters depend much more on brute force and angular strategies. Monsters of my variety, that is. Now that I know at last how we are procreated. If indeed there are others like him and me.

But his face was his mothers, other than the snout. He had a neck ruff with sharp jagged edges and his fingers and toes were bright red talons. I marveled at how he resembled me so much. It was the final clue to my own inception, five hundred years ago.

Since he was so much like me I named him after myself. When Chantel arrived next I told her his name: Hydrophilica. The water lover. Being hungry that day, he sulked. He refused to come out of his cave to greet her.

"Fine," she said. "No problem. I'll come back next month." These visits were hard on her, for every month he was more and more the monster.

He was sulking because I had chastised him for going

down to the camp, devouring every last one of the home-less men and women. He didn't leave one behind. He said he did it not to leave a trace. But I knew it was just a case of voracious appetite. I told him he couldn't fool me. And that he had better get it under control or there would be no fools left to eat.

"There's always fools." He sulked, and went off to hi-bernate for a couple years.

In that time I grew ravenous. I looked at Hydro, sleeping like the dead, and I lost control of myself. I ate him. I hardly felt bad about it. Cannibalism. It bothered me not the least, and when Chantel rode her bike up to the lake for her monthly visit, I didn't even try to hide the fact.

"Gone," I said. "He's no more."

"Creep. You ate him, didn't you."

I just stood there looking at her.

"I'm pregnant again," she said.

But I knew it before she told me. Without really looking at her I knew it, I could feel it under my skin and I knew this one would be a bigger disaster than the last. I knew she would keep on having babies until there was a swarm of us, rapacious and devouring until no one was safe. No one *was* safe as it was, and when we were five or ten strong we would decimate the entire city of Malibu. And then we would move on. My sense of monster ethics was insulted. I had to find a way to stop her. The thought of competing was more than I could bear. I realized then what a loner I was. Lonely, yes, but even more than that I liked being the only one of a kind. I liked being the only real embodiment of evil. Tales of Vampires and Ghouls were what they were but I was the real thing. I did not want to share that distinction with anyone.

She camped out at the lake, waiting to deliver the baby, and no sooner was the thing breathing its first independent breath than I popped it into my mouth and ate it. It went nameless from this world. Three more times Chantel came to me for her deliveries and three times I popped the baby into my mouth and swallowed hard. Animals do this kind of thing and humans are always grossed out by it. Yet it's the most natural thing. Think of Cronos.

But the fourth baby was normal, except for a tail, and her I let Chantel keep. She named her Georgia and she survived although her father did not. He's dead and gone. Devoured. I had to put a stop to her proliferation. And I had been hungry for a Petry for a very long time.

Chantel and Georgia were inseparable right from the start. And I had to worry about that. Because she put Georgia into swimming lessons at the Malibu pool before she could walk. Lying in the tall grass around the pool, spying on mother and daughter, knowing that the tail was curled up in a bulky diaper, I became incensed. I was so angry I slept for fourteen years, waking up just in time for a private birthday celebration between Chantel and Georgia.

I crept into a tree and peered in their bedroom, the room they shared, which had once been Ivory's. They sat together on the canopied bed. Chantel was explaining that, while she didn't have the slightest recollection about her birth date, still she had something to give to her for her fourteenth year, and a mission to fulfill. And that's when I saw her pull up an old crumpled paper bag, and pull out the kriss.

I don't know why I didn't eat Chantel or Georgia any sooner. I am very old now in Monster years and may not even live long enough to finish this tale. My hide is dry and litters the lake with dander the size of dinner plates. My tail has fallen off for perhaps the last time. But I can finish the tale of Georgia and Chantel, how they were inseparable and determined to get me in a vulnerable spot and plunge the kriss into my neck. And yet, how they fell apart, thus losing the strength it took to pursue me.

They fell apart over a man. Chad Petry and Brad Petry were gone from this earth. Chad died of natural causes, surprisingly. He had gotten overweight and developed dia betes. Brad as I said was my dinner one lonely night. But both Georgia and Chantel were attracted to a man named Johnson Jones. He was the lifeguard at the Malibu pool, just a high-school kid, really, but Chantel and Georgia fell in love with him at exactly the same moment, the same day and the same hour, when he climbed down out of his chair and tripped, stubbing his toe on the way to the bathroom. That's it. They both noticed him at the same time and they noticed each other, noticing him. Georgia, fourteen years old, had a rougher time of it since, because of the tail, she could not wear the bikini bottoms that Chantel wore. Geor gia wore cut off jeans and a halter top, and the tail made it appear that she had a hunch, a misshapen bottom. Chantel, in spite of her stretch marks, still looked very good, solid and muscular and yet slim and tanned. One would notice her body anyway, even if he weren't Johnson Jones. She walked with a proud strut, not an ounce of fat on her, tall and breasty with long legs and long, almost simian arms which were delicate and braceleted with bangles from her wrists to her elbows.

I followed them home from swimming every day, just keep ing tabs on them.   They lived almost exclusively in Chantel's room, taking food back with them and sharing meals, even stuffing the cupboards with food so that they would not have to make as many trips down to the kitchen. Dr. Sidhu had simply decided to cope with them. Dr. Sidhu had aged gracefully, achieving the face he deserved. When his children grew up and left him he simply replaced them with others, but Chantel could not get a job; her attitude was her disability, and so she stayed on. The day she brought Georgia home in her arms, Dr. Sidhu threw up his hands and laughed painfully. He was informed about the tail--Chantel, I suppose, thought it impossible to hide the fact. I don't read her mind as clearly as I'd like to but it's a logical assumption. Then Dr. Sidhu adopted Georgia and gave her the Sidhu name, and he let Chantel help the housekeeper as much as she liked with the baby. He was really a defeated man by then. Defeated by Ivory, and then Chantel, and finally by Georgia who grew up to be con-tentious about everything. Even as a baby she wailed half of the time, finding relief only when Chantel came home from school to hold her. As a fourteen year old child with a tail she was stubborn and almost vicious with the other children. Her hormones were raging. It occurred to me that I could risk eating Chantel now. Georgia would be left behind. But first I had to entertain myself a while with their fight over the lifeguard, who in actuality did not seem interested in either of them.

But the day they both spotted him at the same moment, they came home riding bikes, and I followed them at a distance, sliding quadro-pedal through the grass along the road. Even as they rode their bikes there was competition over who would pull ahead, and when they dropped their bikes in the driveway of Dr. Sidhu's house, they faced each other off.

"You're too old," said Georgia. "You're an old lady. He's mine."

Georgia jumped forward and dug her hands into Chantel's hair and pulled, kicking her shins. Chantel screamed and threw her down, jumping on top of her and the two of them rolled around right there in the driveway until Dr. Sidhu came out and threw a bucket of water on them.

"What in God's name!" cried Dr. Sidhu. "Both of you. Come to your senses. What is this about?"

They stood staring at each other, breathing hard and fuming, and as Dr. Sidhu began to repeat his question they flew up and at it again. I left Dr. Sidhu trying to pry them apart. I felt safe for a while. They were too distracted to come for me.

Of course, it occurred to me to eat the lifeguard, doing them both a favor, and he was definitely appealing. I put it off for a while; I was grateful to him. With him in the picture they did nothing but ride their bikes to the pool everyday, to stare at him and prance around the pool, and every day when they returned home they fought. Chantel had a cast on her arm and Georgia had her nose re-set--Dr. Sidhu administered to them himself.

Johnson Jones, the young lifeguard, gazed out over the pool and yawned into his hands frequently. I lay in the grass growing beside the pool and watched the whole scene--Chantel lying out in a skimpy bathing suit at the far end of the pool. Just staring at him. Georgia leaping off the diving board, doing swan dives and jackknifes to show off, maybe to compensate for the funny bulky shape of her behind which jutted out like a hump on her backside. I knew, as only a monster can, what would finally happen, and I wanted to be present when it did, when Chantel tipped fate by getting herself half drowned and calling for help.

She started out slowly--one could see she was really afraid of the water. She moved into the deep end, holding onto the edge of the pool. She looked over her shoulder at Johnson Jones, yawning into his hands. Then she shoved off and began splashing, calling for help. Johnson Jones dove into the water from the lifeguard stand, came up underneath her, got her into a chest lock, and swam her into the shallow end of the pool, where he slipped her onto his back and carried her out of the water. She pretended to be semi-conscious and I almost snorted out loud. He laid her down in the grass and put his ear to her mouth, where upon she groaned lightly, slowly, pretending to wake.

"Don't move," said Johnson Jones. "We have the paramedics on the way."

But Chantel lost control of herself. She reached up, hooked an arm around his neck and pulled him down, planting a wet kiss on his mouth.

He staggered backward.

"Just wanted to thank you for saving me," she said

"Not necessary!" he said, wiping his mouth with the back of his hand.

Over on the bleachers I could hear Georgia cackling, en-joying a good laugh--like a spectator, watching the home team loose. Then the paramedics came and left, and the two women got up and road their bikes home.

The next day I followed them to the pool again. This time it was Georgia's turn. She stood in the shadow of Johnson Jone's lifeguard chair and looked up at him, shad-ing her eyes from the sun. I crept closer so that I could see what was happening. It occurred to me that Johnson Jones, while handsome and tan and muscular, could have been any half naked young man, and that it was the com-petition between them that mattered. I crept up to the patch of grass along the chain link fence and listened.

Georgia was telling him about Dr. Sidhu's house, what chaos there was, how he bought his children any toy they wanted, how they got ice-cream every night. How strangely, everyone got along. Except for Georgia and Chantel. The lifeguard listened to her disinterestedly, keeping his eyes on the pool. Then she asked him. She flat out asked him. *Would he care to go to bed with her?* What did she think she would do with that tail?

The lifeguard stuttered, squirming uncomfortably in his chair. He pretended not to hear her. I could see that I was going to have to eat him, just to stop the two of them from embarrassing themselves any longer.

That was when they first teamed up against me. I don't

know how they knew what I was up to or maybe they just knew me well enough.

I was in my cave and I was hungry, sort of sifting through a pile of bones, looking for an ounce of meat. I became aware of them on the surface of my lake. In a boat. Circling around and around with a fishing line. I surfaced just enough to peer at them undetected. Tied to their fishing line was a baby possum, alive, swimming in little circles on the surface of the lake. Georgia held the line and Chantel stood above her with a machete. Obviously they meant to take my head off.

How they knew I couldn't resist a baby possum was beyond me. But I couldn't resist it. Especially since it was put there by Chantel and Georgia as bait. Especially since their hands had touched the deed.

The trick, then, was to be faster than them. A thing I believed I would have no problem with. I could move supersonically even in the water. But more than that I wanted to teach them a lesson.

I rushed up to the surface of the lake and snagged the baby possum and swam backward just as Chantel tried to lob off my head. But reaching out across the lake she fell in, and had to be rescued by Georgia, who held out an oar, and I pulled the possum and the line and the whole pole down into the lake with me, and I let the possum wonder around my cave, sniffing, looking for a way out, until finally I grew bored and ate her. A day later I waited for Johnson Jones to close up the pool and I ate him, too, leaving his left sandal behind.

I began to worry about Detective Short. What was he doing with all these missing person cases? Was he making any headway with the Left Foot Stalker? Did he have a suspect? Was it me?

Although I thought it might be dangerous, I molted back to human form, to the psychic detective. I went to see Detective Short.

Unfortunately, Detective Short hustled me into an interrogation room.

"Where did you put the bodies," he asked me. "How did you kill them?'"

How many...where...when? He had so many questions!

I scoffed at him. "You convict me automatically? You're not even interested in what I have to say?"

"I'm listening," said Detective Short, and he pushed the recorder closer, since I barely spoke above a whisper.

"Well, it's like this. I molt and change into a rapacious monster. The swamp is my home, and I eat just about anything. But I eat humans most of all."

"So," Detective Short scratched at a patch of dry skin on his neck. I had some guilt about the fact that I was exhausting him.

"You are eating your victims? Like Jeffrey Dahmer? You're eating them?"

"No one can stop me," I said. "I'm unstoppable. I could leave this minute and you couldn't stop me. Or I could decide to eat you."

But I decided to be led away to jail for a while. Jail was a thing I liked. A whole network of angry, irascible people like a stirred up hornet's nest. They made the best eating. So I signed Detective Short's papers--my confession I guess it was, and I let him lead me off to jail.

There I feasted every night. I molted back to my saurian self and slipped through the bars. I ate from the cell to my left, and the next night I ate from my cell to the right. I crawled one floor up, and the next night I ate from below me. I molted back to human form and sat patiently in my cell, feeling very content. Finally I ate the guard on duty, and I slipped into the warden's office and ate him, too. I could have hunted down Detective Short, but him I left alone. I had affection for him. He made my life interest-ing. He pursued me. He always knew it was me. I liked that.

I returned to my lake, leaving the prison in an uproar. When I got home all was in peacefulness. The Monarch butterflies and the dragon flies flitted over the lake. Beavers and opossums waddled about their business. Coy-ote and fox crept to the edge of the shore to drink. Fish jumped in the night. I realized how much I loved my lake. How I had never taken it for granted. How hard it would be to leave if Chantel and Georgia ever perfected their work with the kriss, the one thing which made me feel vulnera-ble. The one thing, the only thing, I knew for sure that could take my life because it had been carved with creative energy. If I found it and got it away from them, what was to stop them from carving another? I was truly sunk. I couldn't for the life of me figure out how to survive such an attack.

I started staying awake at night--no more lovely months of hibernation. Georgia came several times to the lake, armed, I knew, with the kriss. I could feel it in my bones.

But she was waiting for me to surface. She wanted to meet me on her turf, I had to assume, not on my own. Not in the watery cave. She was afraid I could over-power her there, and it's probably true I could.

It became a standoff, Georgia and Chantel riding their bikes to the lake each day, waiting for me to surface, and some days I would surface and sit opposite them, on some rock covered with lichens, waiting for them to make a move. I was in fear for my life but it's also true I was bored and needed them for my entertainment. If I took a step for ward on the shoreline, they backed up. Georgia, holding the kriss at her breast, was breathing deeply and Chantel, at her back, tried to push her forward as she backed away. They got into shouting matches with me, and that was the best they could do.

"You stupid bloodsucker! You bone head! Baby killer!" Georgia quivered all over as she waited for me to become incensed, and then to lunge forward so that she could plunge her kriss into my neck. But I was not stupid. I knew I could count on them to grow weary of this game, and tired of carrying the kriss everywhere with them. They would find other men to fight over, and they would forget me for a while.

I had to make some decisions for myself, in the mean-time. I had always liked Chantel but nothing was more natural now than that I should eat her, leaving Georgia alive for sport. How would Georgia feel about that, I won-dered.

I soon found out. I waited under the window of Chantel's bedroom on a hot summer night. The window gaped wide open--I knew it was to tempt me--knew that she slept with the kriss under her pillow. Georgia slept in the same bed, with her head at the foot.

I slid inside and down the wall and under the sheets. I devoured her while she lay sleeping. So soundlessly did I work that Georgia never woke up. I had my chance then to take the kriss. I looked at it, placed it back under the pillow. I don't know why I did this. Was it self-destructive of me? I wouldn't think an animal would be self-destructive unless things were hopeless, and they weren't hopeless. Was it something from my human side? Did I actually pity my victims?

Eating Chantel was a little chancy. I mean psychologically. When I had eaten Ivory I dipped into self-loathing in a way which could only be human. Now, eating Chantel and then backing off to my cave, I felt cheap. I felt that I couldn't trust myself. Had I really needed to eat her? Couldn't I have spared her, and spared Georgia the grief? I was terrible, I knew, but was I that terrible? Apparently I was. Apparently I would eat anybody, even those I loved.

I felt blue for a while, thinking Chantel was gone from this world, and it was all my fault. Then I got over it. She had been a sufficient meal, and few meals ever left me feeling satisfied. Thus I was grateful to her, and in time I was not sorry I ate her.

I still had Georgia to entertain me. I could try to befriend her, I thought. It just might be possible.

I slid through the grass to reach the bottom of the canyon and then I climbed a tree tapping against the window in Chantel's room. I hissed at the window, seeing Georgia

there studying herself in the mirror. At first she didn't notice me. Then she spotted me in the mirror. Without
turning around she spoke to my reflection.

"You killed her!"

"No I didn't. Wasn't me."

"You killed her and now I'm going to kill you!"

"And just how (I laughed like I was coughing) do you
plan to do that?"

She picked up a thing, I believe it was a coffee cup, and
she turned around and she threw it at me, but of course I
am psychic, so I ducked, laughing.

Frustrated, she turned back to my image in the mirror.
And she picked up another think, a shoe, and she threw it
into my reflection, shattering the mirror, so that when she
looked again I was multiplied by ten, laughing, hissing.

I hadn't gotten to know Georgia. She didn't stand out in
my imagination the way Ivory or Chantel did, and I
thought it would be best to get to know her if she were to
sustain me from boredom. At moments I still regretted
eating Ivory, thinking no one could take her place. I followed Georgia out of the house one day, and when she
climbed off her bike to push it up a hill I slid up behind her.
I stayed in the grass so that she wouldn't see me. But she
could smell me. And she stopped and jerked around.
I watched her fumble with her blouse and pull the kriss out
of her bra. She dropped the bike and began beating the
weeds, looking for me. She followed her nose, and suddenly
we were face to face. I realized I was in a fight for my life,
that each child had inherited the will to kill me, and each
child was stronger than the last. Thus Georgia was strong

enough to kill me. Strong enough to plunge that kriss into my neck and finish me off. I began pleading for my life. She lunged forward and attacked me, riding my back. I flipped and threw her off and ran back to the lake but she pursued me, riding swiftly on her bike. She was right at my tail. I reached the lake and plunged in, turning back to see if she'd followed me. She dropped the bike, kriss in hand, and plunged into the water. I could see that she was a killing machine. But she could not hold her breath long enough to catch me. She could not reach the underwater cave. What a wimp! Even Ivory could do that. Some swim mer! I was both relieved and dismayed. Where was the sport? She swam back to the surface, sputtering and muttering curses. She got back on her bike. Hours went by and I basked in the sun, taking on the look of the lichens on the rocks. I thought I was through with her for a while. I thought of lazing into a nice three year hibernation. But just as I was about to slip into the water I saw her bike reap pear through the trees, and I saw that she pumped the bike with great difficulty--I saw that she carried a heavy load-- the scuba tanks and her wet suit. For once I felt I had met my match.

There was nothing now for me to do but swim down to my cave, to wait for her to approach me. Part of me felt confident. She would be dressed in the wet suit and her moves would be clumsy. Part of me felt that I was breathing my last oxygen.

I sat in the darkest corner of the cave. I heard her plunge into the water, and soon I saw her swimming towards me. She landed at the foot of the cave, took off her tanks. She held not one but two kriss, one in each hand. I lunged, but she jumped forward and blocked me, so that we collided. We both fell back. I was stunned, and she knocked the breath out of me. Then she sat on me, forcing the kriss, one in each hand, pointed at my neck. I grabbed her arms, trying to turn the kriss backwards. She was almost stronger than me. She nicked me with the left kriss. I felt a searing hot burn, and then I forced the right kriss backwards into her eyes and gouged them out. She howled and stumbled back, floating half dead to the surface of the lake. She fell unconscious, and I was in the terrible position of having to breathe life back into her, which I did, and when she sputtered and coughed up swamp water I dove in and floated down. I was in no mood to eat her after that. How she made it home without her eyes I can only guess.

After that, Georgia sat every day in her bedroom by the window. I often went there to spy on her. Though there was not much to see. She rocked in a chair with bandages over her eyes. She sang a little bit. I thought I would feel pity for her but I didn't. I sat in her window and watched her. Finally I talked to her. I apologized.

"I'm sorry about your eyes. But you were going to kill me. I was only protecting myself."

She didn't answer me.

"What will you do now?"

She tilted her head toward me, but still she wouldn't answer. She appeared to be in a stunted trance.

"Can we call a truce?" I asked. "I will promise not to hunt you if you promise not to hunt me."

She twitched lightly . I thought it looked like a death

shock, electricity after the fact. I took that for a yes.

"Good. Fine, well, we can be friends, then. You know, for five hundred years I have been lonely. First there was Ivory, and she was a lovely child but finally I ate her. Then Chantel came along with her song and her spite, and I ate her as well. But now I have you. And we can sit here and ward off each other's loneliness. Perhaps we can even share body heat," I said, for I was truly lonely, and I crept up next to her and rubbed against her feet. It was the most unexpected thing. She suddenly looked delectable to me. And I ate her. And she laughed inside my head while I was eating her. And then I saw the bottle. Succinylcholine! Probably raided from Dr Sidhu's black bag. Perhaps he had even given her the paralyzing poison, to get rid of me. Per haps he was a believer. And because of my digression I realized too late that she had eaten the poison. Knowing I would eat her.

And so I forced myself to regurgitate, but it was too late. I grew violently ill. I wheezed to take in air through a swollen wind pipe. Asphyxia! My body became leaded and thick. In this condition I dragged myself without dignity back to the lake and dropped like a stone, thinking that I would like to die in a place where no one would find me and later stuff me in a museum display.

For three days I lay on the floor of my cave, wrenching and drinking and vomiting and pissing. I actually died and came back to life. I could see that I was truly indestructible. When I recovered I went over to Dr. Sidhu's house, to look for a few plump children to eat.

That's when I first met Dr. Sidhu face to face. I was

perched in a tree which overlooks the swing porch, where he sat with three of his babies, and my goal was to swoop down and leave him empty handed. I meant to do it in a blur, too quick for him to see. I swooped down, all right. But I wasn't myself. I was weakened by the poison, and by the will of Georgia, and when I went to tear one of the babies from his hand he shrieked and came down on my head with his fist. I was so surprised. I'd thought I'd acted too swiftly, but there he was pounding on my head. I slid back into the woods surrounding his house and made it back to the lake. I had really blown it. Now Dr. Sidhu would know that I was real. He would tell Detective Short and they would all know who the Left Foot Stalker was. Me. A Monster. A real monster. They would form a posse and come looking for me. Of course they couldn't kill me but still it would be very embarrassing.

Detective Short would put two and two together and come looking for me at Half- Moon Lake. I didn't have to wait long. He showed up with a crowd of deputies on horseback and a pack of hunting dogs. I asked myself, had I ever eaten a horse? I didn't think I had.

I rose to the surface of the water, with just my eyeballs protruding like a crocodile. They lined the lake all the way around. They sat patiently waiting, and when something stirred they shot at it. I ducked and dove and they spotted me, all of them shooting at once, but a bullet is more of an annoyance with me. It gets into my hide and itches until I find it and pluck it out. I waded down to my cave and plied my talons to pluck at what felt like hundreds of bullets

Every day, every night, there were sentries around the

lake, and Detective Short, inevitably. He never went home. I wondered if they could starve me out. How propitious would it be for me to molt into some human form and just miraculously appear in the lake? That was my only plan and it didn't seem like a very good one. Then, for the first time in five hundred years, I realized there was no other way out but to end the dream. Perchance to wake up, or even dream another dream. And sitting in my watery cave I tried but it was not forthcoming. I was stuck as I am today, growing weaker by the hour as I try to live on silt and fish and the occasional horse and rider that I steal away from the borders of my lake. On pure boredom. When I dream again, I won't be this monster anymore. I will be a girl, sitting pretty at the edge of this lake, fishing and having daydreams of lovers, rich and handsome.